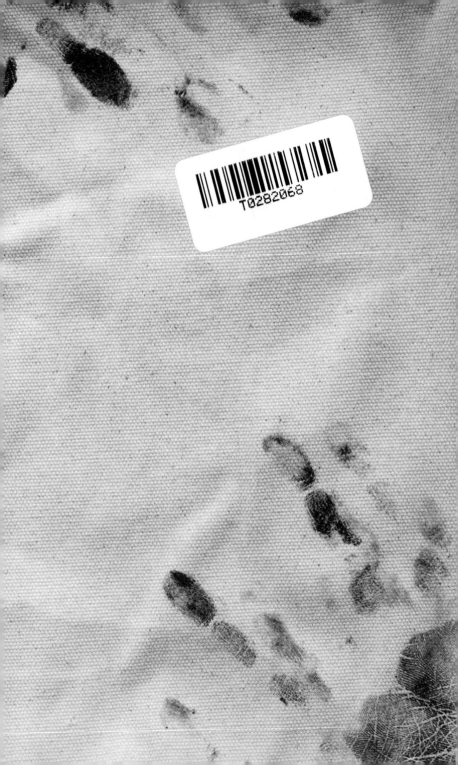

THE
LADY
OF THE
MINE

SERGEI
LEBEDEV

TRANSLATED FROM THE RUSSIAN
BY ANTONINA W. BOUIS

NEW VESSEL PRESS
NEW YORK

New Vessel Press

www.newvesselpress.com
Copyright © 2025 Sergei Lebedev
Translation copyright © 2025 Antonina W. Bouis
First published in Russian in 2024 as Белая дама.

Library of Congress Cataloging-in-Publication Data
Lebedev, Sergei
. . [Белая дама, English]
The Lady of the Mine/Sergei Lebedev; translation by Antonina W. Bouis.
p. cm.
ISBN 978-1-954404-30-4

Library of Congress Control Number 2024935261
I. Russia—Fiction

FIVE DAYS IN JULY 2014

DAY ONE

ZHANNA

Nine. Nine months of her mother's illness. In her memory they were like a sticky clump of stained sheets from her mother's soiled bed, turned into the lair of a wounded animal, after she refused sponge baths. The only thing Zhanna remembered clearly, discretely, was the January Monday, the first Monday of the New Year, when she first wished Marianna would die soon.

There had not been much snow then, barely enough to cover the furrowed fields frozen in the hardened nakedness of autumn plowing. The anxious wind, blowing in sudden bursts from the northeast, quickly blackened it with coal dust from the old slag heap. The heap seemed to be frozen; the cold had it in its clutches. Yet the energetic wind worked hard to blow off the tiniest grains and flakes of coal and spread them over the snowy covers.

First the snows lost their whiteness. Then they turned gray. Grew darker. That always happened in winter—until the deliverance of the next blizzard. But here the blizzard was very delayed, and the snow ended up as a black icy crust that devoured the weak and brief light of day.

Zhanna thought that if her mother had not gotten sick,

3

the snow would have fallen in time to whiten the earth properly. But her mother was sick. Her body, twisted and warped by convulsions, scorched by fever, secreted not sweat but the tarry blood of suffering, which penetrated every fabric, from cotton pillowcases to silk nightgowns, and not just fabric but furniture, walls, the very air of the house, which was already wintry oppressive because the windows were sealed to keep in the warmth.

Belatedly trying to acquire her mother's mastery, thinking victory over stains would mean a small victory over the disease, Zhanna tried to wash the sheets. They would not come clean. The machine swirled water for nothing. Zhanna boiled, soaked, wrung, rinsed, beat them with a heavy wooden roller. But even the resounding blows of the roller, in Zhanna's inexpert hands, only splashed and splattered the blackness that had soaked into the fabric, staining the sheets and house even more.

All her life Marianna had used her strong, dexterous hands to wring the linen. She tortured it, forcing it to shrink into a tight braid, and then spread it out again under the blazing iron, renewed and innocent. And now as if in retaliation, the force of the disease was twisting and flattening her. All the dirt she had washed was coming back, settling in her darkening body and clouded mind.

For three decades her mother, head of the now shuttered mine laundry, wore a white work coat. Above all others, she loved and admired medics as if for the unity of their occupational color, their loyal and professional passion for cleanliness, for their strict procedures of disinfection, chlorine, and boiling. At home, there were no tapes or plasters in the first-aid kit, no old nonsterile bandages, and at the least little scratch or wound—Zhanna hurt herself frequently, "my thin-skinned girl," her mother said—Zhanna's mama would take her straight to the hospital to old Dr. Shpektor for him to wash and disinfect the wound, as if she saw tetanus in every speck of dirt.

This intensified the weepy exasperation with which she implored Zhanna not to take her to the hospital or bring doctors home. It was as if the illness that had taken over her system, self-aware and defensive, was speaking through her mouth. Physicians were no longer guardians of health, sentinels of purity, saviors; they were torturers. Her mother feared and hated them, fearing, Zhanna thought, even the white color of their coats, which had been a sign of affinity. Zhanna did not have the will to insist on the ability to make the right decision, which Marianna used to have in abundance, and Zhanna had grown up inside her protective bell jar.

Left on her own, Zhanna could only adjust to her mother's new, terrible, possessed will, being drawn involuntarily into her madness: discouraged, left destitute by the sudden loneliness and the hopelessness of the situation.

Marianna was respected in the town. But with a coldness, with distance, as if for some reason—although Marianna had never traveled farther than Donetsk, only once to Graz in Austria, as a health aide—they were not sure that she truly belonged, that she was one of them. When the mine finally shut down a little over two years ago, Marianna begged them not to close the laundry, to make it commercial, but in vain; and since then, people seemed to resent her, as if they were expecting her to convince the owners not to shut down the mine. She went to Austria for six months, going to Europe as many local women did, but she was blamed for it, as if she had gone to a resort to have fun, not to change an old foreign man's diapers. Therefore, when her mother fell ill, Zhanna did not have a faithful helper or counselor.

She never told anyone the details of what was happening: she was ashamed to reveal the nasty secret of the illness, to cast a dirty shadow on her mother.

The neighbors and acquaintances, sympathetic in words, gradually distanced themselves. Some dark, tormenting premonition hung in the air. The older ones recalled the months before the July collapse in 1996, in which her father had died, when the mine was warning them of a coming catastrophe: the methane would burst, or the cage would get stuck—stop, it seemed to say, trouble is coming . . . Marianna was never sick. No germ ever stuck to her, not even cold and flu. So her illness became a sign that the usual times were ending, something was going to happen, and people without realizing it had already switched sides to the uncertain future, where there was no place for Marianna.

That January Sunday night, a windless, heavy snowfall began, its apparent silence carrying a comforting, lulling, gentle rustle. Reflections off the fallen snow lit up the rooms, chasing the bruise-like shadows into the corners.

Marianna had fallen asleep peacefully, as before when she fell asleep lightly, gratefully after her labor, after work and her handwashing at home. She took on cleaning things that no machine, either at the laundry or at home, could accomplish, and Zhanna imagined that her powerful body, molded by the washerwoman movements, her hands used to kneading water, creating foam, radiated and gave off an energy, like an engine warmed up after a drive, and the crisp coverlet breathed that energy, filling the house with an unearthly freshness disconnected from anything, a supernatural scent of cleanliness.

Taking advantage of the quiet that night, Zhanna reached Dr. Shpektor by phone and persuaded him to come.

Before they shut down her mother's laundry, the hospital linens were also done there, and before, the doctor's coat glowed with sparkling whiteness that seemed to be able to heal on its own. The doctor arrived in the same ironed coat, but Zhanna noticed that the fabric had darkened, lost its luster. Shpektor himself, pedantic and tidy, had grown flabby and frumpy, as if without her mother, without her laundry, without her daily handwashing the whole settlement was going to seed.

Shpektor used to enter the patient's room confidently, making it known that he was there to conquer. He immediately touched the patient, probing, tapped with his fingers, listening to the body, forcing the disease to respond, to name itself. His fingers, too long for the thin and short Shpektor, were a pianist's fingers—people joked with a smirk that he had hoped to go to the conservatory—and they were his main diagnostic tool. Zhanna remembered how they touched her when she lay in feverish flu, how they transmitted invigorating signals as if by Morse code, and she hoped with all her heart that Shpektor would understand what was ailing her mother and find a cure.

But the doctor had come reluctantly and barely entered the bedroom. He did not touch Marianna, explaining that he did not want to wake her. He's afraid, she realized with a start. He was afraid of the disease. Her hope vanished, making room for fear, all the greater because her mother's illness had become part of terrifying general changes that even Dr. Shpektor could not fix. He led Zhanna into the other room, heard her out, patting her hand—she felt weakness in his fingers, once strong and firm—and he said, "We need a blood sample. But, Zhanna, I can tell you without the tests. It's cancer. It's swift. There is no hope. No one would perform surgery now. And she won't survive chemo."

After a silence, he stood up and put on his coat in the hallway. He shuffled his feet at the door and looked at Zhanna. He opened the door, took a step across the sill. And now as if no longer being in the house made him feel better, Shpektor said, "The cancer moves very quickly. You must be prepared. In a bad way. What you told me, that she refuses to see doctors . . . That's only the beginning. Forgive me. The toxicity is too strong. She will lose her mind."

Shpektor told her what might happen next. Zhanna heard and didn't hear: what he described could not possibly apply to her mother. "She won't recognize you." "She'll think you are her enemy." Didn't he know her mother? There was only a tiny part of her mind that believed him. Believed and feared. She saw that her mother had already changed. From the very first day of her illness.

It was then, after the doctor had left, that Zhanna wished her mother would die easily and quickly. She wished it, because she had heard the women's saccharine "done with suffering" at town funerals. She was immediately ashamed, but she was ashamed reflexively, falsely, superficially. And having realized the pretense, she held her breath as if waiting for the true shame to come, to make her cry, to grieve in her body. But the shame did not come.

She felt—for the first time with such acuteness since the beginning of the illness—only a deep, impotent resentment of her mother. It could have happened to anyone, the neighbor Anya, for example, but not to her mother, because Mama was, was . . . Zhanna, choking on resentment, couldn't find the words to name her mother in her true essence, which few knew, some guessed, but almost everyone felt.

Her mother—before—was protected, enchanted. And her mother was to reveal her secret to Zhanna soon, to explain who she was and what she did while pretending that she simply washed other people's clothes. One day, soon, maybe in a year, maybe months—Zhanna had foreseen it; she had read her hints.

And now she was dying, having broken her silent promise—not given in words, but explicit—having deceived

Zhanna's faith in the grace of her future hereditary vocation, which she was already accustomed to trying on, not yet knowing of what it consisted. She took as a pattern, as a sketch, that strange sense of the special significance of her mother's life that was incommensurate with her work. She ran the laundry and then took in laundry at home in an age of washing machines and detergents, yet some people considered her a healer, others a seer, others a witch, and still others, the majority, simply a wise woman whose advice should be followed.

But all this was off the mark. People tried to capture only the elusive. But it—the magic—was in her mother, in the movements of her hands, in the water between her palms, in the cleanliness of the washed linen, the cleanliness that surpassed whiteness.

It was now a cherry-filled July. The tree outside her mother's bedroom window, an early species, overflowed with cherries, almost black purple, sweet, knocking at the window when the wind blew: the branches should have been trimmed in spring, the trunk cleared of lichen, whitewashed. Her mother—what was left of her—had calmed down, breathing more evenly, as if the cherry tree had found a simple key through its sound to her raddled mind. Zhanna had a desperate hope that her mother would get well, that it was possible to return from such a deadly distance. On those sunny days, Zhanna, sensing the blackness of her thoughts and feelings, the stifling, nasty twilight, the timeless void in which she lived, begged the cherry tree for her mother's recovery, whispered, "Save Mama, cherry tree," without realizing that she was approaching madness herself. She sat at her bedside, looking into the face that had turned into an unfamiliar mask, hoping that the remembered features would flicker, and her mother would overcome the mask and return to herself.

She almost believed it—and slept through the actual death, napping in the next room, missing her mother's last breath.

The body that lay in the bed among the dirty sheets, twisted into frozen suffering, was not her mother.

"Right out of a concentration camp," the ambulance orderly said to his coworker, thinking that she did not hear him, but she did hear, and the words stuck in her mind, as if explaining something.

"Right out of a concentration camp," Zhanna whispered to herself.

When the ambulance left, she went out into the yard, on a bright July day before twilight. She had done nothing there since fall, and it showed neglect, abandonment, but of a special kind. The yard was not overgrown as could be expected with thick and greedy weeds. The grass had not grown. Rather it was stalled, choked with time, emptied and thinned, darkened by the coal dust. The mine had not yielded anything in almost three years, but the slag heap still shed dust. Between the two nearest apple trees hung a sagging and frayed rope where her mother used to dry laundry. There was nothing on it; Zhanna dried her mother's sheets in the house so that strangers' eyes would not read the shameful horror of her illness.

But now a sheet, an imaginary white rectangle that once hung there, a spectral sheet like a window or screen appeared before Zhanna's eyes, forcibly combining present and past, compelling Zhanna to recall the first instant of the end.

She had arrived back from the city, from college, on the weekend, four hours by bus, without warning her mother. She missed her, even though just Wednesday she was planning to spend the time with her books. It was her first year, her first semester. But she was worried by her mother's voice when they spoke on Thursday. It sounded inexpressive and alienated, as if she were communicating from another planet. Zhanna tried to persuade herself that was as it should be; they were growing up, separating. But she could not. She left class, took the intercity bus, believing that as soon as she heard and saw her mother, the fear would dissipate; she scolded herself for the sudden and unneeded trip, chasing away the growing apprehension, like hair rising in the atmospheric electricity before a storm.

She walked from the bus station. She relaxed; she had imagined so many times walking along that road as a student, a city dweller, and here she was, local and yet no longer local, and she had a psychology textbook in her bag. She relaxed, but she was still anxious, as if she had not chosen the right focus of study, not moved to the right city, and it was only in this town that it became clear.

She walked into the yard along the concrete path her late father had made; he was a mine surveyor, a man of precise lines, and the strip was always as straight and even as a school ruler. But it seemed to Zhanna that its parallel edges had bent invisibly, as if something had shifted underground. Although, even after the mine collapse, the path had remained ideally plotted.

This imagined curve had confused her senses; the ground shifted below her feet for a second. Zhanna thought she would fall. Catching herself on the edge of dizziness, she saw her mother.

Marianna had her back to her; she had just hung a sheet on the line. It was the most familiar, the homiest scene; it should have reassured her, returned the ground beneath her feet.

But Zhanna felt that something was wrong.

It was a weekday in autumn. The sunlight had weakened, grown clearer, with the purity of spring water, not yet filled with fading yellow. In that light, which did not know the passion of color, innocent light, Zhanna saw: the sheet was white but not clean. "Cleanliness is superior to whiteness," her mother liked to say.

Zhanna—who with her sixth sense knew that special cleanliness, its radiance that was not born of the nuclear, burning power of detergents, or of the tenacity of scrubbing and rinsing, but of the quiet miracle of her mother's hands—realized that the cleanliness had been taken away, vanished.

Marianna did not see it. Did not notice.

Zhanna did not mention it. Her mother did not seem happy to see her. She sat her at the table. She bustled in the kitchen, and Zhanna could see: her words, gestures, movements—everything had turned somehow unnecessary, inelegant, sloppy. Some dishes were too salty and others overcooked.

Zhanna spent the night, and left, persuading herself that it was all her imagination. She promised to return in a week, but got involved in her classes, and she didn't really want to go back, especially since her mother's voice seemed better, almost back to normal, and she assured Zhanna that it was better to study, work, and then you can come.

What she should have done in those days was drag her to doctors, take her to the regional hospital in Donetsk. Or even farther, to Kharkiv or to the capital, Kyiv. Maybe they could have done something. But when Zhanna returned, her mother was mostly bedridden. Only her voice was still lively. A sly, false voice. At first Zhanna thought her mother was stupidly using the last of her strength to appear better out of concern for her, so as not to distract her from her studies.

She quickly gathered it was something else. Her mother was behaving like a changeling, a stranger afraid of being exposed, and she tried to keep Zhanna away. When she realized that Zhanna could not be chased away, Marianna became cranky and imperious, even though she was physically weak. The change was so unimaginable, as if it was not a change but a substitution, that it bewildered Zhanna, who did not know how to act, what to feel. Marianna would push her away, demanding she move out immediately, or she would beg her to stay, weeping and sobbing but without feeling, like a windup doll, like a madwoman. Zhanna was thrown into fever, into chills, while her mother demanded, pressured, refused permission to call doctors, invite friends, ask for help: "No one, ever."

And Zhanna, at a loss as to whose desires and prohibitions these were, whose voice it was, her mother's or her illness, submitted. She had no time to think of a countertrick. She made up her mind when it was too late, and her mother, sinking deeper into her illness, refused the consent she had given yesterday, becoming even more irritable, capricious, and mad.

The doctors seemed eager to act. "Has the patient agreed to hospitalization? No? Talk her into it! She won't agree? Declare her incompetent." Her mother, seeming to hear it all, even though Zhanna was talking outside, hissed, "You want to send your own mother to the loony bin?"

That blessed snowfall, that visit of Dr. Shpektor remained in her memory as a distant beacon, a light on the abandoned shore. The following days and months turned into a corridor of darkness, into a mine shaft after a cave-in, where everything was mixed and crushed, fused in agony, in the horror of her mother's unstoppable transformation into a mummy, into an alien something, dying and unable to die, as if death enjoyed its time in her body.

Now that her mother was gone, Zhanna felt even more strongly that dark, indistinct mass of eeriness and suffering that remained here, in herself. She tried mentally to free herself, to disengage. But her mind involuntarily returned to the surprised words of the orderly who had seen so much: "Right out of a concentration camp."

The words referred to something else, as well, which the attendant probably didn't mean. To the old, abandoned Shaft 3/4.

There, across the field.

Beyond the slag heap.

To what was in the shaft, under the concrete plug. Superstitiously avoiding calling the contents by name, even searching for a name, Zhanna finally understood that her mother was assigned to this very shaft as a guardian, as a keeper of a sealed well or vessel. And if her mother had died, dirty, lousy, and wasted, it meant that the seal no longer worked.

Everyone in the settlement knew what, or rather who, was in the shaft. It was a shared secret. A compulsory fact, not to be spoken of. Except to be mentioned superstitiously.

She felt the ominous scale of destiny, the power and nearness of fate that had been revealed through her mother's illness and death. She felt it and could not contain it: exhausted, frightened, standing on the line of inheritance. Feeling relief about the death and horror of what she, the heiress, would now face. Lost in lost time, in missed events, locked in a capsule of unexperienced experience. Devoid of the feeling of neighbors, the physical nearness of others— and thank God that they weren't intruding, questioning, that they had left her in peace, digging in their gardens, drying their blue-gray sheets.

Twilight had come. The sun set behind the black, two-humped slag heap, as if falling into the earth's jaws. Time had rushed by, off to somewhere, as if her personal chronometer counted hours as minutes.

She went into the house, empty for the first time since last autumn when her mother had stopped going outside. She remembered with difficulty, in fragments, as if her memory was in some other city and she had to reach for it, that she had to cover the mirror. With dark cloth, she thought.

She obediently opened the drawers of the chest that had blankets and tablecloths, but there were only light fabrics, laundered and ironed by her mother before her illness. Folded into even piles, almost wounding with their aired and impeccably pressed corners. Radiating innocence. Zhanna was afraid to touch them, aware of her dirtiness: body, thoughts, soul. She looked around the house of the past, recognizing its light, its colors, for the first time so obviously convinced that there really hadn't been anything dark in it.

The big mirror used to stand in her mother's room. But in January, Zhanna dragged it out to the living room: she could not bear seeing a doubling of the bed and her mother's crumpled body in it. She had turned the mirror to the wall: she did not want nor could she bear to look at herself, either. She wanted to disappear. Now with nothing to drape over it, she turned it back, with a self-humiliating gloating, prepared to see a dirty dummy, a mocking puppet copy of the dead woman.

What she saw, with a shudder, was a different self.

She had never resembled her mother.

Marianna was tall, as if she had to be noticed. Slender, with the harmony of strength, not beauty. Full-blooded, without cuteness or tender blush. Elegant, not in her features but in the precision of movement and gesture that ennobled her features. Smiling, pleasant, but without warmth.

"Lady, excuse me, are you the last in line?" asked an intelligent old man waiting for milk at the market. Seven-year-old Zhanna remembered, extracted the word out of its shell, the chatter. A weighty, real word that seemed especially appropriate for her mother, revealing the truth of her essence and origins, which no one in their ordinary mining town could have suspected. The more attentive ones noticed that Marianna was not like the other women: the local life had not left a brand on her. The old man, Zhanna suspected, had intentionally chosen the word *lady*. He wanted it to sound like a joke, irony, but it had hit the mark. That day at the market, Zhanna noticed for the first time that her mother was not like the others, even standing in line. Other people seemed to attach to one another, like interlocking toy blocks, they knew that they were a line and behaved like parts of a whole; her mother seemed to be in line, not showing off, but separate. On her own.

A lady.

Marianna.

And what was Zhanna? A girl, a late child. Late in growth and maturity, with a striking name, but she was scruffy, pale, ungainly, as if not of her mother's blood. Only her name promised that one day she would be different, amazing, Zhanna. Like the song on the radio: "A stewardess named Zhanna, beloved and desired."

The dull mirror showed one, preparing to be the other.

It showed how resemblance was coming into focus in the nonresemblance. How in the awkward body on the brink of maturity, not yet a woman's, hints revealed Marianna's fine rich figure before her disease. Her body, crumpled, diminished, diseased, had been taken away in a black bag to the morgue.

But here it was, returned. Incarnated in the daughter.

It's a curse, Zhanna thought, bringing her hand to her face, touching her hair, with her mother's characteristic elegant gestures. A curse.

Her hair! Marianna had thick golden hair; it had gone gray, faded in her illness. Zhanna's was ash-colored and stringy. But now there was a shade of gold in it, gold like her mother's.

She was her mother now. And her mother was just like the ones lying in Shaft 3/4, in the coal depths. That was just how Zhanna had always pictured them. Emaciated. Black. Completely alien.

"Right out of a concentration camp," the chatty orderly had said. The devil made him say it.

She ran from the living room, leaving the mirror uncovered, and with disgust and anger began stripping her mother's bed, tearing off pillowcase, sheet, duvet cover. Aware that she was acting badly, that she should have left the bed until tomorrow, preserving the room in peace and quiet, she could not stop. She pulled, dragged the fabric, knowing that she would not be able to clean away the stains; she had been unable to clean anything these months, even after two washings and boiling, stains reappeared like signs of her impotence and the power of the disease. She made Marianna's bed with the spotty sheets. Silently, silently she damned her mother. Marianna did not have the right to betray her. Dying this way, repulsively and horribly, turned into an obsessed prisoner of a concentration camp. She did not have the right to leave her.

Zhanna wanted to burn the linens but was afraid the neighbors would understand her feelings. She bumbled around the house with the bundle and in the end went down to the cellar.

All the houses in the town had deep cellars; the miners knew how to dig. She tossed them into a corner, covered with old rags and boxes. She took a deep breath, like a criminal who had finally gotten rid of the evidence.

The light flickered. Stone fragments fell from the ceiling and rattled onto the floor—as if something big and threatening had passed through the stone walls.

Zhanna climbed out of the cellar and went outside. Nothing. There was a smell of burned diesel fuel. Maybe a truck or combine had driven past?

The sky was clear, and a bright dot moved among the stars. A plane. Zhanna used to watch that heavenly path in the evenings—an international route passed right over the town, an airplane highway. Up there, above fields, houses, and slag heaps, there was almost always someone there, someone flying overhead. Zhanna, who had flown only twice in her life, used to feel a joyous fondness and friendly envy for the passengers, who did not know about her looking at them, head thrown back, from the earth. It was as if a short-lived spectral connection had been made, and for an instant they became locals, friends—and then flew off into another life.

But now there was only angry bitterness. The plane, at its ten thousand meters, reminded her about everything that had been blocked by her mother's suffering. The war. The Russian troops that had moved in stealthily from the east. Her college that remained in Kharkiv beyond the front line. She was stuck here; she had missed her chance to leave when it had still been possible.

She sat on the stoop, in her favorite spot, the second step on the right, and watched the flight for a long time. She wanted to be on it. She wanted to be like a cuckoo and push out the soul of one of the bodies seated on the plane, to steal their destiny. There she was, Zhanna, in a window seat, feeling that she was moving away, no longer her double on the ground, and the plane was taking her over the edge of the horizon to meet the coming day.

The airplane vanished, dissolving in the sky.

She felt something, as if someone had caught her thoughts, caught her unawares. She looked around—it was quiet, empty—and hurriedly went inside.

VALET

Zhanna closed the door.

All right, Valet had seen all he wanted. The neighbor girl had grown up—time to get her in bed. But he wasn't thinking about her now.

So the old bitch had died. Died. Suffered a lot. Paid for everything. And how she died! She was so fastidious. And she turned into Baba Yaga. Really. Into a monster, a zombie from the movies. And most importantly, in time. Just in time. As if someone had heard Valet's secret wish and made it come true.

He felt avenged. But not completely. He smoked, standing in the tall, dense blackberry bushes that overhung the fence separating the neighbor's front garden. This was his observation point since childhood: he used to break through the blackberry bushes, as if hunting for berries, and, hidden by the foliage, he would lean against the decrepit fence, observing their yard. Watching, indeed, peeping at Zhanna.

He was still feverishly shivering when a Caterpillar-tread vehicle had driven by the house a minute ago on the village bypass road. Other people would not have realized in the twilight what it was. But Valet recognized it: an Omela surface-to-air missile system. A SAM. He had seen it uncovered at parades in Moscow, standing in the cordon. A pair of missiles covered with a tarpaulin flashed in the dim light of a streetlamp, and it seemed to Valet that it looked like an erect dick pushing up a cadet's fly. All this—Marianna's humiliating death, which had trampled her beauty and dignity, her secret power; Zhanna's shivering, naked loneliness, left unprotected; the deadly SAM system, which was not officially here; the troops, which were not officially here; he himself, who was not officially here, either, he was allegedly on vacation—merged into an exhilarating cocktail of power, revenge, winning, surpassing everything he had experienced in the police special regiment.

Valet could not fully believe his good fortune. Last December, when there was already movement on Maidan, Uncle Georgy, the commander of the special regiment, called him up and told him that Valet had been selected as a volunteer—his uncle grinned at that word—and that he would soon be going home. He would go in civilian clothes, for all outsiders to think he was there to visit his mother.

Valet almost said he wanted to stay. Good thing he bit his tongue. Otherwise, his uncle would have pinned him to the wall with questions, questioned him about the real reason. Uncle knew how to interrogate. And he would have thrown him out of the regiment and disgraced him in front of his fellow soldiers.

Of course, he would: a man afraid of a woman.

And Valet, though he was in the army, and went out to confront the crowd in a helmet, with a shield and a club, was afraid of Marianna. He was afraid, that's all. From childhood he had sensed in her an alien will and magic, witchcraft, which ordinary people do not have.

His mother did not tell his Moscow uncle Georgy, a lieutenant-colonel, the brother of her crippled husband, why Valet had to leave his native home immediately. She told him about Valet's father, maimed by the collapse. About the mine that is on the verge of being closed. That she didn't want the boy to inherit the dangerous life of a miner. And if he stayed here, in the future he'd have to go to the diggings, to makeshift, shallow mines, to the places where coal was extracted illegally and where they didn't live long, because they saved money on the bracing, or didn't put it in at all.

Uncle Georgy, who was so distrustful, believed it. It was almost true what his mother had said. That's why his uncle thought that Valet would be glad to return: to show his former motherland who was strong. For his uncle, the Marat coal settlement had never been home.

The family came from an impoverished Voronezh village. In Soviet times, the older brother went west, to the Donbas, as a driller. The younger went east; he stuck to the capital after the army, in the police service. The year 1991 split them apart: one became a Ukrainian citizen, the other Russian. The brothers did not like each other; the older thought the younger useless, thought waving a nightstick around was easy. The younger thought the older was a fool—who else would labor in a mine, ruining his health? They did not visit, occasionally called on holidays. But his mother also sent parcels secretly, containing this and that, some homemade pickles. And those pickles paid off.

Childless Georgy regarded his nephew, Valentin-Valet, as a son, happy to take him into his breed and change him. Valet was happy: his mother knew only that Georgy was in the police, which is why she sent him her son to have the foolishness beaten out of him. Georgy turned out to be much more than an ordinary officer; he was in a special police regiment that broke up stupid demonstrators. He organized Valet's documents, expedited citizenship. He got him into the army, not under his wing in the interior troops, but in missiles, in a remote and harsh area, sort of like a test. After that, he took him into his own regiment as a private.

He liked Valet. Georgy trained him, didn't give him special treatment, but promised just another year or two and you'll go to officer school, you'll be an officer. His uncle was waiting for his promotion to colonel, and then general would not be far off: "We'll find you the right wife, from a police or prosecutor's family."

But there was just one thing he couldn't understand: why Valet never went home on leave. Valet would hem and haw; sometimes he was sick, other times he had training courses—he couldn't tell his uncle that the neighbor in charge of the laundry had chased him out of his own home and forbade him to return. She told his mother that he should never set foot there again, and his mother obeyed. He obeyed, too, because he knew that if the old woman Marianna said something, so be it, and it was better not to cross her.

Just take Vasily Three Heads, a tough miner who was the number one bully. Falling cobblestones in the drift had struck his helmet on three occasions, and his brains were fine, hence his nickname. He used to harass the girls at the laundry. At first, Marianna tried to keep him away with words. That didn't help; Vasily was stupid and a bit deaf.

What happened next, Valet saw for himself; his mother had sent him to borrow some detergent.

Vasily was drunk. He was on a rampage, rattling the tubs. The girls were huddled in corners; Valet froze in the doorway, unable to leave or enter, he had seen Vasily in fights, he was powerful and terrifying, the locals had broken more than one cudgel on him. Yet Marianna came out to meet him calmly, and lightly, almost jokingly, she slapped him in the face with a wet, freshly washed towel.

The intoxication was knocked out of the tough guy, the bull. He staggered, grabbed the doorframe, turned white, and sank to his knees, as if a battering ram had hit him. From then on, he was docile, he forgot the way to the laundry, he forgot about fighting, and he took up raising chickens and ducks.

The main thing, Valet sensed, was that the slap with the towel was just for show, a trick, for Marianna's power was much more than that. The rest didn't get it. But he did, he had watched her for a long time, they were neighbors. It was a two-family house, one end facing east, the other west, porch to porch, life to life.

As a child he had wanted Marianna to be his mother. His mama was a cleaner at the mining office; Marianna was boss of the laundry. Both cleaned, but their lots were different. His mother washed scuffed floors, polished them, emptied the trash, worked hard, and came home filthy, despised. Marianna washed away the miners' toxic dirt, but came home looking as if she had been embroidering all day.

The fathers were good friends, a blaster and a surveyor. Valet often went to the neighbors' side as a boy. He noticed his home seemed to be tidier, not a speck of dust, as if his mother was trying to prove something to her neighbor, but the neighbors' place was cleaner, though the floorboards were not so shiny, and the windows were sometimes cloudier. It was there, in the neighbors' half, that Valet felt a chill: as if Marianna could see through him, every black spot inside, every mischief, every lie. Seeing but not judging. Yet. Then he dreamed that he was sitting in a trough, a brat, and Marianna was soaping him, running her fingers through his hair, whipping up the foam, running the brush over his back, over his shoulders, his chest, his arms ... But suddenly, the brush skipped and Valet could feel that something black had stuck to his hand, glued, eaten into the skin, he had not noticed when or where, and the brush began rubbing it, harder, more painfully, and it wouldn't wash away, and the brush was tearing his skin, making it bleed, and it was still there.

He woke up: he looked; his hands were clean, but there was a bruise rising as if he had been rubbing it with his fingers.

He grew older, his father had been crippled by the collapse, Marianna's husband was killed, and he began to notice that while Marianna let him into their house, she did not welcome him. As if she was protecting her under-age daughter, although what was there to protect. Nothing. Kiddie jokes, Masha and Vanya, sitting in a tree, k-i-s-s-i-n-g. There were loads of silly rhymes like that every year. Valet grew up resentful, and his resentment made him learn to see people clearly. He understood that Marianna had a future ready for her daughter, measured and cut, in which Valet, the kid next door, could have no place. Valet vowed that it would be the opposite—he made the vow out of naked resentment, out of anger, and he stopped visiting because he was afraid that Marianna could read the secret in his mind. It was only when she was not home and Zhanna came in from school that he would go into the yard, so that he was visible from their house, to dig in the garden, chop wood, sensing the little squirt looking at him. There was a five-year age gap, he was almost an adult to her; they weren't classmates.

The child's dream was prophetic. That's how it turned out. He turned sixteen, another year of school left. That's when the nickname stuck to him: he used to be Valka and became Valet. Because he liked to play cards, the older kids taught him. Valet in Russian was the Jack in the deck. He was lucky at cards, the Jack of Spades helped him out, it appeared as if he had ordered it. He ruined other people's hands, even though it wasn't the most powerful card.

His crippled father, through his friends, got him into a digging pit. At first only as a handyman, to turn on and off the winch that pulled the wagon up on the rails, made from an old bathtub—the usual mine wagons couldn't fit in the pit, it was too narrow. And to be honest, he never wanted to be a miner, and after his father was cut down and crushed by a rockslide, he became afraid of the underground.

He had worked for two and a half months, and they said to him, "You seem to have the skills, and you have the muscles. You'll go to the rock face." One of the men there had been hurt by a collapse, his leg broken in three places, ribs compressed until they cracked.

The depth there is nothing—thirty, well, maybe forty meters—the pit is arranged in a ravine, so as not to dig too much, and it reaches only to the very top layers, where the coal is garbage, cracked; if you look from below, you can even see the rays of the sun in the mouth.

He went down, cut and chopped the coal, and listened: How would the rock respond? And his father, a paralytic turned to stone, who shat and vomited what seemed to be liquefied coal dust, loomed before his eyes, and Valet was ready to do anything to avoid ever coming down to this site again. But where would you go, there was no other work, the whole district was riddled with mines. Engines puffed, winches turned, trucks carried coal—someone big was behind it, drilling the earth with other people's hands, shaking its black udder, knowing how to substitute grades and documenting second-grade as first-grade . . . They dug without a clue, just to make a fortune, while the miners had to use bad coal for heating in winter, and the old people scavenged on the slag heaps, looking for anthracite, left over from previous times.

After his third day in the digs, he turned to the abandoned Shaft 3/4. It was not far away. His feet led him there. They didn't play there as children, shepherds didn't drive the cattle there; it was a bad place. As a boy he had heard their fathers talk about the 3/4—they said it was the deepest, the widest; it was once intended for coal lifting, for bringing out a mountain of coal. But it was sealed with concrete from above and cut off from all the mine levels underground, "corked like a bottle," his father used to say, because *they* were there.

As a small child, Valet thought that *they* were the military: a secret mine, and in it a secret missile, the biggest in the world, left over from the USSR, one that could destroy the whole of America with one explosion. Valet imagined a whole underground city where the rocket's maintenance men lived. He imagined how it was assembled underground, how spare parts were transported by a secret underground road from the east, from Russia. He imagined how one day the lid of the mine, that concrete one, would rise, and the rocket would show its gigantic nose, red, necessarily bright red, and come out of the ground, tearing, pushing the coal seams apart with the power of its engines to crush the enemies across the ocean.

At sixteen he naturally did not believe in the rocket anymore. He learned what was really there. His father told him.

The Jews were there. The ones the Germans killed during the war.

His father didn't like Jews. According to him, they had disrupted strikes before Valet was even born, and they were to blame for the collapse that had crippled him. His father was fixated on the story that the Germans had taken gold from the Jews, rings, watches, and teeth, putting it in a wooden box at the edge of the mine. And one Jew, the last to be thrown in, kicked the box down the mine. If they couldn't have it, nobody could. It was village lore, a crazy story, but his father was obsessed with it. He kept imagining how he would be cured if that gold could somehow be dug up, taken from the dead, it had to be shallow, since the last executed man had pushed it down.

Valet didn't believe his father, of course.

But the thought of the gold crept up on him: What if?

A forest had risen there, young poplars, yellow and red leaves carpeting the ground, even though it was mid-August, with swollen warts as if they had been scalded with acid. It was too busy: red, yellow, yellow, red, purple, crimson, yellow, crimson again, and the color so bright, too alive, like a splash of real blood. His head spun with fatigue, with the color patterns that shifted kaleidoscopically, his legs did a drunken swirling dance. Valet fell. He woke, blinked several times, the light was fading, creating strange shadows through the poplars, like figures sliding, flowing.

He looked closely—something was peering at him from beneath the leaves. He lifted a leaf carefully: a strange pebble, like a coal crumb but with an unusual shape, not like pieces of coal, it was too rounded. He rubbed off the soot and greasy coal dust, and there was a flash of hot fire.

Gold. A small nugget, the size of a pinky nail, smooth like a newborn.

Valet picked it up with his left hand and laid it on his right palm. It had weight. Real gold.

Naturally, he knew that there was no gold in these parts. He was a miner's son, after all. There wasn't and couldn't be. Wrong geology. So, it wasn't natural. Not a nugget.

It was that gold. Jewish gold.

He looked closer.

The piece was crumpled, like a used bullet. If you straightened it out mentally, smoothed it . . . It looked like a tooth crown. His father had them. Four teeth. He got them in the Soviet days, with his bonus. The mine collapse had squashed his face, twisted his jaw, crushed them. Those gold crowns remained in the mine. Oh, how his father missed them! The mine had taken everything from him. If he could pull them out and take them to the pawn shop in the grocery store lobby, he'd have money, like *Heberews*—that's how he said it, *Heberews*—who had hidden their gold.

Valet held the crown in his hand in front of him, like a divining rod.

He walked slowly, moving leaves with the toe of his shoe, peering into the slag. Nothing. But he had the feeling that they were around. Nearby. One, two, three of them playing hide-and-seek. If he found them all and took them to the shop, it would be so much money: farewell, digging; farewell, dirty mining life. The longer he looked in vain, the more gold teeth his imagination painted: ten, fifteen, twenty-five, forty.

He had mining fever, a mania, when a person thinks they will break through the empty rock any moment and will open a rich layer, trace the vein that goes off into the depths, beckoning with its tail like an elusive snake. But in fact, there was no stratum at all, and the vein was long exhausted. But the possessed man believed that the emptiness, the absence of signs, was the surest sign that the mountain was playing with him, and in the end would surrender and open its depths, so he pounded and hammered until he fell, exhausted.

Valet found a rusted shovel without a handle and began poking out a furrow. Tomorrow, tomorrow he would come with a pickaxe and a good bayonet shovel; he needed more than one furrow, everything had to be dug, checked, before somebody else showed up, some tramp.

Valet dug thoughtlessly, angrily. He thought that he was seeing into the depths, and some shadows were smiling at him from the lower darkness with golden smiles; disembodied figures on whom golden things glowed invitingly: watches, bracelets, spectacle frames, rings, earrings, chains . . . He had already buried himself waist-deep in the ground when suddenly he heard, "Treasure hunting? Can you dig up a cigarette?"

A tramp did show up. A stranger. A gray, greasy-haired, stubby old man with a soldier's shoulder bag. He would take a day's work and steal what was lying around. To him Valet was just a boy, a teenager. The vagabond was not afraid. He was curious about what was going on here, he could smell Valet's excitement and passion, he wondered if there was anything to be gained there.

"What did you find there, kid?" The tramp came over, looked into the pit; he obviously knew something about this place, he knew about the gold teeth, Valet thought, he knows, he knows, and when the stranger, having made up his mind, reached out to Valet to grab him by the chest and shake out the secret, Valet whacked him across the face with the blade of the shovel, once, twice, a third time, and pushed him into the pit.

Strange: the body took up a third of the hole, but the soil still fit into the hole, all of it, without any left over.

He tamped it down. Covered it with colorful leaves. It was deep. The animals wouldn't dig it up. No one would come looking for him. He dumped the shovel in the fire pond on the way home.

He meant to examine his clothes carefully at home, even though they were covered in coal and earth, to see if there were any bloodstains. He took off his jacket and pants, threw them on a chair, lay down on the bed for a second, and passed out.

And slept for a day and a half. When they came from the digging site, his mother said he was sick. She started washing his work clothes. She changed the water three times, but some stains wouldn't come off no matter how hard she tried. She went to Marianna, who was also doing the laundry. "Help me, like a neighbor, my devil got so filthy in the digs, no powder can get rid of the stains."

Marianna took the clothes. She brought them back the next morning. Ironed, still smelling of the iron. Clean, but not quite.

The dirt had come off, but the blood was still there.

And she put a crumpled gold tooth on top of the pocket. She stared in silence.

His mother also looked at the stains that even Marianna couldn't wash away.

Valet stared, too. He couldn't understand: what was a dream, what was reality, whether there had been a tramp or not . . . Only the golden tooth attracted his gaze against his will.

And Marianna said, "Pack his things for the road, Anna. He is never to set foot here again." She stamped her foot on the floor.

And his mother, though she was stubborn, obeyed without question.

After six years, he was back.

He returned fearfully. On the one hand, his uncle's orders. On the other, Marianna's word. She flung him out like a puppy, the fastidious bitch, by some right he did not understand. Of course, she did give him a new life, but it hurt that the life was built on a lie, and he couldn't tell anyone that the neighbor lady pushed him out of his own house and he can't get even with her.

He didn't tell them he was coming. He thought he would stride through the gate proudly, to say I don't give a damn about you, neighbor, or your ban. But it turned out that he squeezed through in the twilight, creeping so that the snow would not squeak, so he would not be seen through the neighbor's window. He walked into the entry, smelled his father's familiar stink of coal shit, and realized that his mother would kick him out; she would not go against the neighbor. There was no room for him here, in the whole village; even if he dug a cave in the ravine, they would chase him out of there, such was Marianna's power.

His mother ran out of the kitchen when she heard noise in the hallway. Her face was filled with such evil triumph, joyous and evil, that he was no longer afraid and opened his arms, and his mother hugged him and whispered tearfully, hotly, "Come in, come in, Valechka! She's dying, the witch, the Lord took pity!"

That same evening, still somewhat unsure what to believe and preparing excuses like he was there just for the day to see his mother, he crept under the neighbor's windows. There was a small gap in the curtains. He looked just once, and an incredible joy filled him. Marianna lay on the bed, naked, darkened, horrible, and Zhanna was bent over her, in a white coat from the laundry, with a damp cloth.

Those two bodies, one half dead, disgusting, the other ripening, tender, hit him so hard that his hands found his fly and brought out his cock.

As a teenager he used to jerk off seeing their underwear hung up behind the house, wanting but not daring to spill his cum, the mining jism, on it. He jerked off in unison with the surrounding area, drilled with mining holes—now he was excited and quickly splashed on the window frame, the wall, drained by his impossible luck: the mama was dying and the daughter had grown, oh, how she had grown.

It was then, as he shook sperm off his right hand into

the snow, smelling its sour, fermented odor, he understood fully that it was no accident that Uncle Georgy had sent him here. Something was coming, huge and horrible, and he was part of it; it had broken Marianna, and it would give him the daughter, like a loan with interest.

His orders were simple: wait. He waited. Zhanna, it seemed, didn't even know that he was back. Later, in late February, the order came.

It had started: people's vigilantes, rallies against the Kyiv junta, seizure of the administration and police, a militia battalion, roadblocks on the roads to the west where Kyiv troops were, trucks with weapons from Russia, the first battles nearby, sounds of artillery salvos . . . He thought about whether to stop by and see what was going on with Shaft 3/4, but there was no time. And it didn't matter now—there was no criminal case, no search, he himself had gone through the captured police archives.

He would sometimes spend weeks away from home. He saw lots of things. But when he returned, he went at night beneath the neighbors' window to look at Marianna rotting alive and her daughter tied to her by hopeless familial duty.

There were lots of girls. He had loads of money. But he wanted this one, white, clean. He sensed that Marianna had not told her about him. Maybe she meant to when the girl was older. Too late.

He had often thought that he should hurry his revenge. Ever since the war started, he could take Zhanna by force, any day. To whom could she complain? But he waited superstitiously for Marianna to die. He wanted Zhanna to trust him—that would make it sweeter.

And now smoking in the blackberry bushes, he imagined how tomorrow morning he would knock at Zhanna's door and offer to help her—funerals were a lot of trouble. And how she, confused, lost in time, would agree, giving herself to him without knowing it.

He tossed the butt, stomped it out with his foot. He turned around.

Far beyond the fence, in the field, on the road leading to Shaft 3/4, a car's brake lights glowed red.

"They must be taking girls to a party," thought Valet. "They must have appropriated the car."

He already knew the exciting smell of expensive cars seized from their owners.

THE GENERAL

The driver slowed down, sharply steering the jeep to the right side of the road. General Korol woke up from his slumber and looked ahead: Why on earth would Semyon give way to someone? There was no one senior to him, a major-general, in this area, neither in the army nor in the FSB. And even though there was no flashing light on the Land Cruiser 200—conspiracy be damned, all these "militiamen" and "volunteers" had already memorized the make and license number—they respectfully let him pass, although they squabbled among themselves. Every week there were accidents and shootings over who took precedence. They didn't care about the cars—they were someone else's, taken from the local businessmen—but they had a lot of attitude; everyone wanted to be a Napoleon, everyone called his gang at least a battalion or, even higher, a brigade . . . And Semyon gave way only to tanks, and not always. He knew how to drive so that everyone on the road could tell what an incredibly important person he was transporting, and the mechanics and drivers of the tanks were provincial boys who knew you don't mess with black jeeps.

A military monster painted in camouflage pattern on caterpillar treads, with two shrouded missiles on top like a hump, was heading straight at them without turning on its headlights. A surface-to-air missile system. The soldiers had sneaked in their own toy. No disguise at all, idiots.

The SAM roared past, releasing a cloud of greasy black soot that settled on the jeep's windows. The general grimaced, as if the soot had splotched his face. It was the same way the town had greeted him almost forty years ago, when he had started his service here in the district department of the KGB. He had put on a white shirt to report to the personnel officer, and during the short walk down the street from the hotel his shirt turned gray, and his face appeared covered in powder. It was the dusty slag heap. His mentor in operative work was Major Anikin, who met him with the words: "How did you get in, son? Your last name is Korol, king. A monarchical, anti-Soviet—one might say—surname."

The general felt that he was drawn here, to the town of long ago, yet did not want to come into physical contact with it, to walk along its streets, to breathe the blue-gray air, to mix with people, to touch the past and the present.

When the general was summoned to the Lubyanka and informed he was being taken out of the active reserve, removed from his sinecure as director of security at the television broadcasting complex, and sent to the Donbas, he was alarmed: he dreamed of long-forgotten operational games, the search for foreign agents. But he stopped himself: What are you, twenty years old? Haven't you played enough? He wanted to refuse, to blame his health, to say it was necessary to give way to the young, he was the wrong age, his experience was not the same . . .

But the lieutenant-general, deputy head of the service, preempted him. He explained why Korol, who had started in those parts, was being brought back and appointed head of a freelance unit. To inventory the archives. There were operational archives of the Ukrainian secret service, the SBU, seized in district offices and district departments, which they had missed, not taken out in time or destroyed, burned, erased from hard disks. They needed an evaluation of their security, the state of operational records. Especially the records of agents. He was to determine the priority candidates for reenlistment, take safe houses according to the lists, assess the prospects of their further use.

Then the general remembered the archive room of the district department in Marat, remembered the old prewar iron door painted green, iron shelves with yellow folders. He looked around this archive room in his mind, thinking that everything in it had probably remained the same, the door, the shelves, the folders. He sensed the familiar power hidden in those unprepossessing folders and computer files. His fingers felt all the strings that stretched from them to agents, confidants, to keepers of conspiracies, objects of operational development. He felt their fear; they already knew or guessed that the archives had fallen to the Russians, unexpected guests from the East. Who fled, who hid, disappeared. Who obediently waited and were ready to serve their new masters. His former agents could still be alive. They had forgotten about him, did not know, did not feel that he might return.

And the general realized that he was getting excited; he wanted to feel the tension of these threads, like a fisherman: the tension of the line, to experience how those who were caught were beating, fluttering on it. But then the thought slipped deeper into the past. He remembered the obvious, which had receded into the depths: that there, in the Ukrainian archives, there were also Soviet-era cases. Not all of them, of course: some of them had been hurriedly taken to Russia, to the archive storage in Kuibyshev; some of them had been destroyed on the spot. But some survived. They were stored indefinitely, he knew for sure; he had maintained contact with a couple of former colleagues before he was transferred to the active reserve. His own files were in there. His first steps in the service, his youth, his rise to fame.

The temptation to meet with his former self overcame inertia and fatigue.

An experienced playwright of operative art, a master of staged scenes, skillful in choosing the right stimuli and creating the supposedly natural pressure of circumstances, pushing a person to the decision needed by the Chekists, the general felt himself the object of someone else's game, someone else's narrative. But he could not and did not want to resist this exciting bait, sincerely grateful for the appointment, although the security instinct, which had been dormant for years, had awakened and signaled in full force—don't do this, refuse, it's a trap, a setup, someone or something was luring you, as you yourself had lured others.

As the car drove him home from the Lubyanka, the general looked at the familiar Moscow streets, the Kremlin towers crowned with red stars across the river, and sensed with unusual clarity the capital's power, which lay not in its architecture and monuments, but in the layers of the earth, in the embers of old fires. He suddenly realized that during all these years spent in Moscow, at the very throne, he wanted to return to the Marat settlement, to the Marat mine. Where he, a mining engineer by training, was in his element. Where he was left with unfinished business, an unsolved mystery, an unidentified enemy.

But he could have stayed there, Korol thought for the first time. He would now be a Ukrainian general. And corrected himself: no, he would not; he earned the rank of general in two wars against Chechnya; if he had sat around in Ukraine, he would be a colonel, at most. Korol was transferred to Moscow by order of the Union Committee, had been quickly pulled out of Donetsk in the fall of 1991, when the Ukrainian Committee had already been dissolved, when the archives had been gutted and evacuated. Of course, he could not have imagined then that he would never return, that Marat village and the mine would soon be abroad, in another country.

But he always felt their existence, their presence in the world. When he read about the accident in 1996 in the newspaper, he thought instinctively, "They must have touched the 3/4 shaft, the idiots." He could see the Ostankino TV tower from his office window, all its five hundred and forty or how-ever many meters, and thought, Shaft 3/4 shaft is deeper; you can lower the entire tower into it, and there would still be room. When he went down into the metro, he compared its depth, too.

He thought about what was in the shaft. The old borders had collapsed. Rubles with Ilyich on them became worthless, turned into candy wrappers. Coats of arms and flags were gone. Everything was new. Except for the Jews in the mine, under the plug. The eternal Jews: he repeated the old joke. Unchanging, like a gold reserve.

Today, when he got his first break, he ordered Semyon to take him to Shaft 3/4. The same road he'd taken thirty years ago from the regional office. Along the edge of the settlement, past the corner house of Marianna, the head of the mine laundry, the subject of the surveillance operation called "Snow White," which he'd opened. He based it on the religious line, that she was a sectarian, because he could not write the truth in official papers.

However, it had begun with suspicions of religious ille-gality. Their informer, "Tatiana," a neighbor, a cleaner at the ore department, told him that some ladies from out of town were coming to see the laundry chief, as if to visit, but were behaving conspiratorially. Korol wondered, couriers? Back then, they were looking all over the Donbas for a clandestine Baptist printing house. And this fit the bill: a corner house overlooking a country road, with a cellar... He identified the visitors.

Colleagues in their hometowns checked their records: both women had positive files, no relatives who had been arrested, no compromising data on them. They were also laundry managers. One from Karelia, the other from Siberia. From distant places, camp regions. Who the hell knew, maybe they met at some work event? At a seminar on machine washing? He sensed something strange about these visits. The ladies came from far away, not on a business trip, but at their own expense. Why? What's so interesting here in Marat? The mine?

That's when he started a surveillance case. Allegedly for illegal religious activity. He felt that maybe he was wrong in the letter of the instruction, but right in the spirit; there was something religious in Marianna, that is, supernatural. The surveillance team watched her. Correspondence was monitored, phone wiretapped. And nothing: all empty, all smooth, too smooth, as if she were a skillful scout who sensed the surveillance and lived so as not to give the slightest suspicion. She was a shock worker, awarded prizes, winning socialist competitions in laundry. Her mother was a military nurse, from a poor family, recipient of orders and medals, father unknown. And he felt that Marianna was special, not like Soviet people. He thought that he discovered a new sect, where Marianna was like the Virgin Mary, some secret sisterhood, going back centuries. But what the hell was this sect? A washerwomen's union? His colleagues would make him a laughingstock.

And then he figured it out. During perestroika, they decided to erect a monument in the small Siberian town where one of the visitors came from, and *Ogonyok* had a big article about it. There was an NKVD execution site on the riverbank, thousands and thousands of people buried there, in a pit, an excavation. Here, there was a mine shaft. And Marianna, "Snow White," as he dubbed her, was here. She was connected to it somehow. But how? And how to prove this connection? How to figure out what it was?

He did not dig up anything, and the miners' strikes began; he had to shut down the surveillance on her, so as not to distract the operational forces. The general had already given instructions to find that file in the archives. He was sure it had survived. He himself had taken care of it thirty years ago, transferred it to special storage. However, he did not have time to take it back to Moscow. Sometimes he recalled it as one recalls love letters to a woman who did not reciprocate your feelings: with resentment and jealousy.

And now, delaying the pleasure, he imagined how he would lay out this file before Marianna. Would give her time to read it. Page after page. And he would ask her: Who are you? And if she didn't answer, well . . .

Back then, in Soviet times, he could have summoned her for a preventive conversation, pressured her. He could have arrested her, tortured her with interrogations, threatened her. But he was sure in advance that she would endure, as many others had endured. But now . . . Now he could send her to the basement. To the basement of a long-closed sports center, where people quickly learn to answer questions. Now any secret was as accessible as a highway whore. And that's why he was in no hurry; a confession happens only once. Sure, you could set up a video camera, play the tape afterward. But it's celluloid, ersatz, it won't replace the live feeling: shame, despair, with which a stubborn person timidly begins to speak.

Semyon has already checked on the captured databases: she lived at the old address. Together with her daughter, Zhanna, born in 1996. Her husband died the same year, 1996. He died in a collapse, which the general read about in the newspaper. Made a baby, and adieu. The general remembered him. He was good at his profession. He was well respected. But in the family—and these things come out first when working on a case—he was an extra. It was as if Marianna had adopted him instead of marrying him.

The general went over the details of the past, flaws, misunderstandings, dead ends, enjoying the feeling of a vicious circle, which would disappear as soon as Marianna talked. And suddenly it seemed to him that the undeclared war, the seizure of Crimea, the invasion here, in the Donbas, had also happened so that he could return and finish what he had started.

The jeep drove past Marianna's house. It was a prewar layout; the Marat mine was considered a model mine back then, and they had built these two-family houses for the workers. The light was on in the corner room of Marianna's half. A woman's shadow flashed behind the curtains.

Mother or daughter? "Mother," the general said to himself. The daughter was at a dance somewhere, eighteen years old, she's that age. Or away studying. The daughter did not interest him.

The car turned into the field, rocked on the bumps. Semyon switched on the high beam, bright, silver, shining, not at all like the faint yellow light of the off-road vehicle that Korol had driven here thirty years ago.

Boom. A muffled thump, the windshield cracked. The general crawled between the front and backseats, waiting for the next shell or mine to hit. Was it a random raid or had his car been targeted, tracked down? He pushed his shoulder into the door, scrambled out onto the road. And saw ahead, in the headlights, a bloody roe deer scraping the ground with its hooves. Only now he remembered how roe deer galloped, spooked by the vehicle , throwing up their hindquarters: they always came at night to the landing next to the road. That meant he had completely forgotten it, forgotten their running, their shining eyes, and he had forgotten many other things that could not, like roe deer, jump out across the road, stun, and shake his numb memory; he had forgotten something important about this place, about Marianna, leaving himself only the thirst for revenge and possessing her, ever elusive, escaping.

"Shall we go back, Mikhail Stepanovich?" Semyon asked.

The roe was silent. Only its eye, huge, with an amber rim and a coffee-grain pupil, looked as if it were already separate from the head, as if something much bigger were leaving the roe deer, something to which the roe deer's body served only as a shelter, and it looked at the general without anger and fear, knowing that it would not die completely. "Keep going." The general shook himself off and got into the car. "You'll replace the windshield tomorrow."

When he had been here, the concrete covering Shaft 3/4 was nothing but a black patch on the surface. The above-ground structures were demolished after the war when the concrete was poured and coal slag tipped over the top. They tried to plant trees a few times, but, apparently, they had tamped the slag too tightly; those poplars withered at the root. The Moscow experts from the special department of the Tenth, the Department of Records and Archives, who came to inspect the site, always recommended "creating a soil cover, planting greenery." But they didn't have the equipment or the seedlings. This black round spot of extinguished rolled earth stuck out, as if the trunk of a giant petrified tree cut off flush, rooting deep into the ground.

The capital commission ordered him to create plantings. But the area already smelled of kerosene and strikes, not a time to think of green spaces! He ordered more poplars from a tree nursery; a truck brought them to the site, pathetic stunted twigs, and a tractor scraped up some soil.

He expected to see the same slag-strewn wasteland in the headlights. But the car came to a low forest. The trees that he had planted, the stunted weaklings, had survived and started to grow. The general was confused, as if encountering the effect of someone else's will and presence. The same effect he had felt in the old days. Leaving Semyon by the car, he walked around the circumference of the former shaft.

There are thousands of dead Jews down there. How many exactly was impossible to establish; Germans left no precise records of execution, as required by the NKVD. Masses. And one more. Not alive. But not dead.

A ghost? A spirit? The general tried to avoid such words, redolent of mothballed old women's superstitions. This was something objective.

It took the general a long time to find a name for it. In operational work, he never used pseudonyms according to a template, never used platitudes like "Renegade" or "Parasite," which could be found in the archives of any district department. But the name eluded him. And then he grabbed a top-secret Cheka file on the mine. He burrowed into the volumes of the twenties and thirties. He sensed that he was there, that his colleagues were paying attention to him.

And he thought he had figured it out. The one who had designed and built the mine. The one who had died in it. The one known as "The Engineer" in old agency reports.

Korol never said a word about this search to anyone. Sometimes he thought he was going mad: there were no signs that *he* existed. Only a strange, lingering feeling that sucked at his heart: someone was in the shaft. Buried in the depths, but looking as if he were standing next to it. Someone who saw it all and remembers it all. A witness, an impossible, afterlife witness.

The first time Korol felt it was when the commission arrived. Scientists, discussing their own stuff, groundwater, the strength of concrete. And Korol suddenly clearly felt that all of them, the secret people, conducting their secret check, were in someone's field of vision, captured and remembered, and there was no escape.

"Hello, engineer," Korol said loudly. "Here, I've come to visit you. From Moscow."

The abandoned mine was silent.

THE ENGINEER

Ghosts have no life. No present. No past. Nothing happens to them. They are just a snag on a record, a glitch in time.

But I am not a ghost.

I am a fossil.

Petrifaction.

Have you ever seen in a museum or, say, on the seashore, where the waves have undermined a limestone cliff, a two-winged brachiopod shell or the articulated shell of a trilobite? A lifeless shell in which, however, one can recognize a being, the being of a symbol? Ghosts borrow their flesh from the imagination, for the former flesh has turned to dust. Fossils are material: in them, as in letters, in hieroglyphs, mankind reads the book of being.

Once upon a time, among other sciences of earth and time, I studied paleontology at the university. I was learning how to distinguish between a number of extinct creatures, inhabitants of the Elysium of evolution. I studied the bestiary of natural history, a comprehensive roster of monsters, transcendentally distant, that can come to life only in Conan Doyle's *The Lost World*. Alien, ridiculous, horrible, unable to adapt to the changes of the world, destroyed because their hereditary features suddenly turned into fatal flaws, they seemed to me to be the spawns of the spontaneous creative will of nature, which can reach the peaks of beauty only by a selection of lower forms, only after having exhausted the stock of all the ugliness, disharmony, and dead ends of development.

Now, looking, so to speak, from the other side of the picture, I see in those fossils of Homo sapiens, the victims of recent history who have dropped out of the race of evolution, whose skeletal carcasses are crucified and displayed on supports in museums to gratify the human sense of superiority, a certain affinity with my comrades and me.

We, like them, are a mass of absence, of extraction. Removed from the limits of everyday life, I am an object of alienation and negation, as constant as the passage of time. Actually, the constancy of this negation, its pressure, is what gathers us into a semblance of the whole, gives us a semblance of "we," a hint of afterlife.

The idea of evolution, of natural selection, which gave birth to eugenics, fits all too well with the worldview of the average person, who believes that he is alive because he is better. And with those who died in historical cataclysms, there must have been something wrong; they were unlucky enough to be born under an unlucky star (such as the star of David), and so their demise is sad but not tragic; their oblivion is natural.

Therefore we, the culled, are what is not. What is beyond the power of the imagination, beyond reason—far beyond the border of nightmare, beyond the territory of language illuminated by the streetlights of banalities.

The execution ditches and pits, the crematoria of concentration camps can be seen, can be imagined. But we, imprisoned in the mine shaft, cannot be seen, cannot be made an object of imagination: imagination stumbles on us; we are too black, too merged in the materiality of the unimaginable.

We are measured in weight and volume. We are measured in cubic meters, calculating our number by dividing the total volume of the mine by the volume of the human body. And the longer we stay here, petrifying, the harder it will be to bring us to the surface, because we are squeezed, soldered, joined together. We become, as a geoscientist would say, a stockwork, an ore body. The result of a rock formation, of a geological process. We'll have to be mined, like coal.

Thrown into the permafrost, the corpses of prisoners of northern camps freeze in incorruptibility. But if the warming suddenly comes, they will thaw and pass through the decomposition of organic matter. But we are no longer organic. We are imperishable in another way, like stone.

If we were loaded alive onto a train, we'd take up hundreds of freight cars. The dead take up less space.

We have here the world's tightest human community, the ideal of Soviet "compaction," the apotheosis of the communal apartment. Yes, we are as cramped as the gut of an imploding nuclear bomb when the crimping charges have already been fired.

We're fossils.

Useless fossils: not a good joke, but I've never been much of a wit.

Some have been strangled and burned.

Some were shot, buried in a ravine, then dug up and burned, bones thrown into a bone-crushing machine.

We are the Jews of prewar Europe preserved in stone.

Something beyond memory. Alien, like a meteorite.

It's impossible to believe in us. Tell the story, and the first question is: Is it true?

It's impossible to remember us, because it's impossible to remember hundreds of meters of dead people.

Under us lie Red Army prisoners shot by the Germans. Beneath them, people shot by the Bolsheviks when the Red Army was retreating, and the prisoners of Soviet prisons. Under them, people executed in the Civil War by advancing and retreating troops, Whites, Reds, Greens, random people, hostages. Below them, the murdered strikers of the first revolution, in 1905.

Stratigraphy. The tiers.

Unity in fossilization.

As I said, there is nothing ghostly about us. We are too real. Monstrously real.

But what can we be called? What are we? A deposit of human beings, over which, like over the iron ores of the Kursk magnetic anomaly, the compass begins to go astray? A moral compass?

A substance? But what substance? There is no name for it in any language. Hebrodite? Jewspar? The philosopher's stone of the new century, the pure substance of silence? Something like the magic chain of Gleipnir, which, as we know, the Norse dwarves made from the stomping of cats, women's beards, roots of mountains, bear sinews, the breath of fishes, and the spit of birds—something that no longer exists in the world?

We are the mute horror of the European subconscious. Its deepest cellar, where, as in a leprosarium, the unhealable past is locked away. That which can neither be named nor repaired.

Sediment.

Residue.

A lump.

We are now as natural a part of the world as the bones of dinosaurs and mammoths, as dead shells of vanished seas and petrified wood.

I remember how my father, a paleontologist, used to take me to the forested spurs of the Alps in the summer, where on a sunny day a limestone rock overhanging a stream would suddenly show white among the trees, like a screen on which the prehistoric past would reveal itself.

My father would take me to the limestone to see one particular layer, made up only of fossilized shells, mollusks. He would start explaining, waving his hat, that this was the trace of a catastrophe: maybe a meteorite fell, maybe a volcano erupted and changed the climate, maybe a sudden epidemic started. I couldn't speak: it was more than pity; it was an unspeakable dark foreboding clutching at my heart.

If in a million years we are found by a more advanced

life form, what will they think? Pestilence? An epidemic? A falling meteorite?

Abandoned to fossilization, we are placed in the planet's Big Time, in a merciless prehistory. Historical man disconnected himself from the animals, invented a detached death, walled off by rituals of grief. And suddenly he returned to his animal forebears, died like them, cumulatively, impersonally, and was imprinted only in matter. We are in the same register, the same sequence of evidence, as the imprint of a horsetail in shale, the fossilized relief of the surf, a shell sash, the skeleton of a shellfish.

I remember how once in the mountains, my father, moving his hand over a layer full of shells and lecturing me, suddenly froze, as if a blind man who read something special with the pads of his fingers. His attention was attracted by the protruding curl of an ammonite, and he put my hand to the ammonite as well, as if he were playing out the biblical episode with Thomas, exclaiming, "Look! Here is the true mystery! It is Hilosepatis, beyond doubt Hilosepatis, it has such characteristic transverse grooves! But it shouldn't be in this layer! These are the sediments of shallow, almost freshwater lagoons. And Hilosepatis lived at the bottom of deep salty seas, Prof. Ritzer has proved it magnificently!"

My father took a long-handled hammer and a faceted chisel with a sharp point out of his knapsack and put them on the grass.

"Look," he exclaimed again. "We draw precise time scales, build floors of epochs. We describe species. But existence has irony. This Hilosepatis seems to have been placed here on purpose, so that the scientist knows his limits. Of course, we can assume that the surf carried the shell to shore, a storm carried it into the shallows of the lagoon. But that's fantasy, an assumption stretched too far, whereas strict knowledge tells us that Hilosepatis shouldn't be here."

My father put the chisel to the rock, tapped it gently once, once more, and again, slightly turning the chisel, and Hilosepatis separated from the rock and fell into my palm.

I stood silent. Heretical thoughts swirled in my head.

What if there was a God? What if he arranged all this in advance, created all these shells, and was ridiculing my father, while my father chattered on about the "irony of existence?" What if this Hilosepatis, deliberately sticking out of the rock, was theodicy?

I was sixteen. My father saw me as a paleontologist as a matter of course. He even named a fossil lily after me, Erichea, and often talked about the not-too-distant time when we would go on expeditions together.

"You have a good eye, son," he would say. "You are a man of stone. You can read it, though you don't know it yet."

But the world of the frozen past, that fascinated my father, frightened me. In my father's obsession, in his passion to search for what had not yet been found, free from classification, to name it and imprison it in a museum vault, I sensed the breath of a darker passion: the passion to own it indiscriminately, to make the once living finally dead.

Inwardly, I was looking for creation. I wanted to create

for people who needed bread, rights, and freedoms, not ante-diluvian shells. My father was a baptized Jew, and therefore a loyal, even too loyal, servant of the Kaiser. In his speeches at academic celebrations he cleverly managed to draw a direct link between the discovery of an important fossil and the greatness of Germany. Sometimes it seemed to me that he perceived his endless trek, his foray into the past of the Earth, as a colonial conquest in the interests of the Reich: you cannot be late, you cannot be deceived; otherwise, you will show up when people are putting on their hats, the best tidbits snatched up by others. His trips to Africa, to the newly acquired colonies, from which he brought boxes of finds that he had no time to sort through, only strengthened my latent alienation, my dislike of his zeal, the greed of a conquistador.

But in my last school year he took me with him to the Ruhr, to the coal mines, the creation of which had uncovered rare specimens of fossilized flora. I think he sensed my nascent leftist sympathies and wanted to educate me by showing me the dirt and sweat of labor, the rudeness and insignificance of the workers.

But he miscalculated. The miners, the uneducated underground people, aroused in me sympathy and anger against their oppressors. And the mine itself... I suddenly saw what it could be: it was like a creative epiphany, a mirage arising from the stale air and the flickering golden lights of the headlamps. The mine was narrow, black, raw. And I saw it wide, dry, light as an avenue. I heard the measured breathing of compressors pumping fresh air into the farthest drifts. I saw cleanly dressed miners descending into the cages; mighty tunneling machines raking coal seams with their steel jaws; the underground cornucopia, generously bestowing mankind with the riches of the subsoil. It can be said that I had already imagined it, the Mine of Mines, a reverie that was later embodied in the ill-fated Shaft 3/4.

I went to study to be a mining engineer. My father accepted it. He secretly believed that this was just an erroneous path, and one day his beloved fossils would call me, waiting there all the time, in the rocks. After finishing the course, I worked in the Ore Mountains, in the Silesian coal mines, but everywhere I met only the stubbornness of the owners. They wanted to follow the old designs, to dig the same mole holes as before, and I began to wonder if I had been deceived. Maybe it was not too late to return to the hereditary field, to go to Africa with my father?

In 1899, the board of the joint-stock company rejected my next project, the most elaborate and daring.

"Do you want to dig to hell, young man?" asked the chairman, running his finger straight down my drawing. "I don't think the devils would like that."

That night, Rekubratsky found me at the hotel. I was already very drunk; I looked at the empty bottle and saw in it the image of the shaft of my failed mine: its perfectly rounded shape, the hoped-for formwork, the movement of the lifting mechanisms, the glitter of the miners' lanterns. And the glare of smoky restaurant lamps on the bottle glass . . . Had it not been for this picture, I would not have spoken to Rekubratsky: I had always had a strong sense of loyalty to my employers, and he represented the competition, the new French-Belgian society working in Russia.

But the bitterness of disappointment won. Rekubratsky, himself a good-looking engineer, a tall, handsome brunet, that evening was wearing a black suit with an anthracite silvery sheen. I've never seen such a fabric since, as if it had come out of the hands of the seamstresses of the foothills. Shiny black boots. Brilliantined hair combed away from his face. Black eyes that knew subterranean darkness. He appeared as a messenger of Gaia, a divine messenger, and laid copies of my blueprints on the table. Drops of spilled wine immediately stained them red, but I paid no attention.

"I'm glad those fools rejected your project," said Rekubratsky. "They don't deserve you. Even if they had said yes, they would have changed their minds halfway through. We won't change our minds."

The next morning, we boarded a train together, eastward, to Warsaw. To the Russian Empire.

Thus began the journey that turned me into a conditional Hilosepatis, a fossil out of place, out of my stratum. Do you remember how I began our conversation? We are no longer flesh, we are substance. Our former bodies have no name. And yet I ask you, have you ever sensed an undying spirit in the bones of the past? In dinosaur skulls? Something that lingers beyond death? Something that is left behind as if for edification? If so, you may understand my essence.

We are imprisoned in the embers, in the remains of a bygone age: ashes encased in ashes. In the Carboniferous sediments. Oh, it was a strange world, a vestibule world: Pangaea was preparing to divide and form the continents we know, the quadrupeds had acquired five-toed limbs; our world was begging to appear in the old.

But the old trees had not yet rotted: fungi and bacteria did not yet know how to decompose lignin. The wood was buried, eventually giving birth to coal to feed our stoves and furnaces. Our corpses didn't decompose, either: a strange rhyme.

We are placed physically deep in the earth, in the sequence of its annals. Ripped out of the Quaternary Period to which we belong and plunged into the Carboniferous. Before us: the Cambrian explosion of skeletal fauna, the explosion of life, the explosion of diversity. After us, at the end of the Paleozoic, the Permian mass extinction, the Greatest Mass Extinction of all time, as the British say. Nobody knows why, but within literally tens of thousands of years—minutes on the geologic clock—three-quarters of all living species became extinct. The Great Dying, there's an expression for that.

Surprisingly, I used to utter those words thoughtlessly, with even a kind of delight, a scientific enthusiasm, a romantic piety before the catastrophe. Now when I look at things from a fossilized perspective, I do not understand how I did not hear then the voice of fate in these simple words: the greatest . . . mass . . . extinction. . . of . . . all . . . time.

People who live near us, around the mine, know about us. But I wouldn't call it an abstract knowledge. It is, rather, an effort of alienation. An effort of not remembering, even as the person knows what not to remember.

As a matter of fact, I shouldn't have to wake up and speak. Decades of slow hardening, of turning to stone had deadened my spirit. My forerunners, my kin, the *Flying Dutchman*, are condemned to wander, to move without rest, to be endlessly and fearfully awake; this is their torture. Mine, on the other hand, is to be part of the dead mass and not belong to it at the same time; to want to separate and not be able to, fading away at the slow, turtle-like speed of substances.

I was awakened by the war that came from the East. Its sounds: the shots of guns, machine guns and rifles. Back then, seventy years ago, everything began with them, too: with the cannonade approaching from the West. And it ended with a long, monotonous sequence of shots at the entrance of the mine. A long one, with a pistol round per man. Soft, as if fake, as if joking, these claps bounced around the mine shaft, mixing, reflecting from the walls, giving birth to a sharp, menacing echo.

The stone was saturated in this echo.

DAY TWO

ZHANNA

Zhanna was awakened by an annoying sound. *Tick-tock, tick-tock, tick-tock*, rattled her grandmother's round-faced alarm clock. She remembered that she had been winding it all these months, but she hadn't heard it, hadn't noticed its progress, as if the time inside of it had been idle, fake. And now she realized, it was going again.

Tick-tock, tick-tock, tick-tock. So simple and familiar once, the sound startled her.

If she couldn't remember its ticking, how much else was gone? Memories? Habits? Feelings?

She ducked under the blanket, lying still in the darkness, listening to the clock and the frequent, intermittent, unfamiliar beat of her heart.

It felt like the clock was ticking differently than before. Faster. More insistent. The very *tick*, the sound of the second hand shifting, grew louder, with the echo of a clanking gun bolt. She covered her ears with her palms; but instead of silence in her head, she heard the steppe wind howling over the slag heap.

Sitting by Marianna's bedside, she used to think peace would come when her mother died. At least emptiness.

But the despair and resentment toward her mother only increased, as if with her death, her betrayal became finally evident, irrevocable. Ashamed of her bitterness, trying to find the right thread of remembrance, Zhanna tried to call up the memory of the former, healing, soothing image of her mother, which used to be always nearby, easy to call upon. But it did not respond. Zhanna felt that the image was not yet completely disembodied, still existing in her consciousness, but buried under the heavy layer of black days. Only her mother the mummy, her mother the madwoman, her mother the reanimated corpse from an abandoned mine, stood readily before her eyes.

Zhanna tried to create light, to imagine some kind of light in the darkness of memory. A candle. A miner's lantern. But the imaginary match went out without lighting the wick. The bulb flickered on and off. And then she imagined Marianna's hands. The area between them, hidden by foam and water, where purity was born.

That space between her hands glowed faintly, and Zhanna was drawn into the pearly shimmer, into the growing, boiling cloud of translucent, iridescent foam; it seemed to touch her face inflamed with tears, wash her eyes. Zhanna suddenly saw women, as if they had gathered for a wake, all the women, old and young, who came furtively, guarding the quiet female secret from the male gaze, to Marianna in the laundry or at home: Help, save me, wash this. I can't do it myself.

Only the worst stains went to Marianna. The spoiled expensive things, gifted Polish carpets, wedding dresses, city jackets, great-grandmothers' shawls and scarves, trophy silk bedspreads. They went secretly, for it damaged the housewife's reputation to seek outside help, and Marianna did not like publicity; she did not need it.

They came to her with the nastiest, most corrosive dirt that clings forever, which the best dry cleaner in Donetsk could not handle. The prized possession was completely ruined, dead. You would remember all your life how you created that stain, what you spilled, how dirty it was—unless Marianna took pity on you and washed it. It was like going to confession, because an indelible stain, occurring at the most unfortunate hour, on the eve of a wedding, say, or before a birthday, always carries a hidden guilt, a hidden meaning. It seems to expose something. A person guesses its meaning, why it happened to them, why now.

There were others who came, widows, divorcées: they brought bed linen, underwear, on the eve of a bedding, a wedding night or a night of love—let it be clean. Let it be clean. Sins removed. Don't let the sheets remember other previous loves.

Zhanna looked at it, remembered reverently, breathed evenly and deeply, but suddenly the connection was cut off, and, like a screen saver, there appeared the sheets, devoid of the blessing of purity, that her mother had been hanging out on the line when Zhanna arrived in the fall. Her memory began to falter, twitching, producing clumped, crumpled, repetitive images.

Back in the fall, her mother—who had never cried,

always saying, "Water belongs in the trough"—had become teary and weepy in a week and began repeating the same stories with empty, verbose enthusiasm.

How Zhanna's grandmother and grandfather met when he was sent on a business trip from the Donbas to Transcarpathia in the first year after the war, to get lumber for the mine. And they met on a bridge over a mountain river, on which the timber was being rafted. She, a girl of nineteen, washed the laundry of soldiers in the hospital, where enduring war wounds were being treated, washed uniforms, sheets, bandages, pus and blood, sweat and tears, and the soldiers, joked her grandfather, recovered faster wearing the underpants and shirts she washed. The hospital was being disbanded, and she was getting her last payment. He had gotten filthy on the logging trip and had to wear dirty clothes, and she said to him, "Why walk around soiled? Let me at least wash your shirt, the sun is hot, it will dry in no time . . . " He brought her to the mine, where they needed a washerwoman.

Familiar fables from childhood. But now her mother told them with a disturbing persistence, stuttering, faltering, forgetting what came next, and then starting again the next day. Then for the first time Zhanna felt not sympathy but fear and dislike. Her mother could not be so pathetic, so helpless, so slipshod. Or it wasn't really her mother anymore.

Her mother, persistently telling her story, stammered more and more often, catching escaped words with her tongue on her parched lips, and her breath smelled of rotten belching. She looked dazed or blissful, as if doubting who she was and where she was.

Zhanna would have been able to empathize longer with another person, weaker or not so intimate. But her mother, turning into her opposite, acquiring the low traits and qualities she had spent her life despising in others; her mother destroyed her own good image with such relentlessness, purposefulness, and seeming determination that Zhanna reflexively responded with loathing and disgust.

Trying to find a rational explanation, a logical formula for the disaster, Zhanna thought about the carcinogenic coal dust, against which her mother had fought all her life: the dust won, took its own. But the dust was too insignificant, too inexpressive for the image of evil, and Zhanna slipped into incomprehension, whispering, "Save my mother," to the unknown. But she knew in her heart that it was an unbearable desire to return everything to what it had been. "Save my mother" really meant, "Don't do this to me."

And the quiet persistence, the firmness of her mother's character turned into willfulness, into malicious stubbornness. She didn't want to go to the hospital, clutching at the bed until it was too late to take her. She didn't want to eat. She didn't want to drink. She knocked over plates and glasses. Begged to let her die, and then looked at her with suddenly angry, vindictive eyes: Did her daughter obey, did she believe the request?

Zhanna, bewildered, had waited too long for a manifestation of the magic that had secretly surrounded her mother.

Waited for something higher, something she served, to come to her aid. And then, when it became clear that there would be no help, she blamed her mother for her vain hopes, as if she were an impostor, a deceiver.

Marianna, as if reading her worries, suddenly became very watchful, duplicitous, like a prisoner hiding escape plans from jailers. She spent hours watching television, which she used to turn on once a month, endless newscasts and talk shows screening the smoky, orange-lit barricades of Maidan. The satellite dish picked up channels from both sides of the border. And Zhanna noticed that her mother switched more and more often to Russian channels, savoring bloodshed, violence against civilians, getting excited, her hands fumbling, smiling at the announcer, wanting to say something.

Zhanna did not have the strength to delve into what was happening in Kyiv; during the previous Maidan uprising she was a child and remembered it vaguely in terms of the moral poles of the event, because many in the town were against the "oranges"... But now she physically felt where the evil was coming from, because the Eastern broadcasts were confusing her mother's already darkened mind, filling it with poison.

She tried hiding the remote control, but her mother, who could barely move, still found it, as if she could smell it. She took it away once, and then her mother attacked her for the first time. Scratched her hand with sharp nails, which she did not let Zhanna cut, grabbed the remote control, turned on a foreign talk show. Her weakened mother had moments of sudden, terrifying strength that seemed supernatural: Where could such muscle power come from in an exhausted body? Zhanna guessed that it was the power of the psyche, the power of fears, that did not consider the possibilities of the body; she was already afraid of Marianna.

She saw that in her mother's mind the events on Maidan Square were connected with her illness, gave some explanation, a key unthinkable according to common sense.

"Nazis! Maidan! Junta! Coup! Banderites!" the announcer spat out. Zhanna recoiled from this onslaught, unable to understand his nonsense, but her mother seemed to understand, and, being on the same wavelength of madness, listened with dark and cruel attention. Zhanna pictured these words pouring into her mother's consciousness, destroying the usual connections of things and phenomena and building new ones: phantasmagoric and sinister.

Soon after, coming from the store, Zhanna began to find her mother waiting at the door. At first she thought that Marianna was counting the minutes until her return, and considered it a good sign. But Marianna was indifferent to her, letting her into the hallway, barely noticing her; she was waiting agonizingly for someone else.

Zhanna remembered then her childhood fear. Two or three times in her life, when her mother had been away for a long time, and there had been unpleasant autumn nights, and the rain had crept in, she had felt her loneliness, felt the branches of the trees outside the window creaking and rustling in a special way, as if someone were picking a lock. She was afraid to go to the door, but overcoming her fear, climbed on a stool and looked into the emptiness of the yard. She listened to see if there was someone breathing there, around the corner of the wall, who knew that she was standing at the peephole, and who could look through that peephole into her very soul, into the salty, tearful depths of her fears.

The door, sturdy and reliable by day, seemed to Zhanna at night to be deceitful, duplicitous, ready to swing open just like that, to pull open the iron tongue of the lock at the appearance of the one who had power over keys and locks, like the secret art of the snake charmer. And Zhanna was ready to open the door herself, if only not to be tormented by the horror of waiting . . .

Her mother was ready to open the door, to let in what she was waiting for, because she could not stand it any longer, Zhanna realized.

"Come, come, Mama," she said, stroking her tense hand. "There is no one there."

She had made a mistake. She should have just taken her away affectionately and calmly. And the words "no one is there," overly hurried, overly confident, smooth, only confirmed her mother's fear. It convinced her that Zhanna knew that someone was there. She knew, but she was lying.

Marianna gave her a pained and reproachful look, in which misgiving mingled with suspicion: Was she not at one with whoever was hiding in the shadows of the courtyard? But Zhanna, not yet realizing the mistake, suggested in a reasonable and businesslike tone, "Let's have a look, shall we? Let's open the door and see?"

Marianna had never hit her before.

The blow was clumsy, the way children fight, trying to poke her in the side with a sharp fist.

Zhanna let go of her hand in a daze, and her mother shoved her again, pushing her away from the door, and whispered hoarsely.

"Don't open it!"

Zhanna pulled out her keys and quickly closed the main "night" lock with three turns. With each turn of the key, her mother settled down, as if her inner tension was released; she collapsed, leaned against the wall, as if she had totally forgotten what had happened, and Zhanna took her into her room.

In the following days everything repeated itself. Zhanna got used to it, though did not understand how her mother had been sleeping quietly, almost without breathing, yet found the strength to get to the door and stand guard. But then she guessed that sleep renewed Marianna's energy: the illness, like a skillful executioner who wants to prolong the torture, gave her time to recover.

Vague shadows of words fell from her inflamed tongue, unfulfilled whispers—the names of the people or the one behind the door—speaking the language of sleep that the waking cannot understand. Like dead babies, they were born without saying anything.

But one day her mother spoke.

She was at the door again. Her eyes were crazed, glassy. Head tucked into her shoulders. There was something of the homeless beggar about her, fake, theatrical in the faded fox collar thrown over her shoulders, a grim concentration, a prophetic obsession, and the strange dignity of a mendicant with a mournful mind, worried that someone was trespassing on her magpie treasures: wrappers, old corks, a newspaper sheet with a portrait of a handsome movie star, a bronze plumbing valve, a bent fork, a beaded purse, a scattering of Soviet copper kopecks, and a vial of iodine.

"They're there," Marianna said somehow confidingly. "Fascists."

The shock made Zhanna drop to her knees and hug her mother's legs. She babbled, "Mama, Mama, what is it, what are you saying, there are no fascists." And Marianna, with a strict, ritualistic, courtly gesture, as if the chief lady-in-waiting were punishing a misbehaving page or jester, took her ear with her fingers and began to twist it painfully. Zhanna froze. Her mother looked down at her aloofly and said with a vague, gentle threat, "Fascist!"

This word, so strange, so out of place in her mother's mouth, once spoken aloud, seemed to open the door to the next stage of her disintegration and madness.

Whatever Zhanna did, washing the laundry, watering the flowers, preparing a vegetable stew, or shaking out the doormat, her mother inexplicably saw in every action evidence of deceit and conspiracy against her: Zhanna was preparing to move her to a hospice, to put her in a hospital by force, to sell their home secretly. And Zhanna, telling herself that it was the voice of madness, nevertheless gave in, hid at the cry: yes, I want to send her away; yes, I want to sell. Involuntarily the resentment and anger grew: they were the only feelings she could experience; the others seemed to have burned out and shut off.

One day she came home to find people in the hallway. She recognized her former teacher, but she barely understood her explanation that they were conducting a door-to-door canvass, a referendum on independence. The sharp, bright light of a May day, pouring in through the open door, mercilessly exposed the details of their hidden life: the stained papers with no-longer-needed doctor's phone numbers on the table by the phone; her mother's old, out-of-fashion shoes on the shelf; her coat, unworn this winter, saturated with gray dust.

The light seemed directed at her mother. She stood leaning against the wall, wearing an old robe patterned with faded daisies. Unkempt, unwashed that morning, she didn't realize what she looked like. Her eyes stared with a beguiling, eerie clarity. The painted, perfumed girl in the gold rhinestone blouse listened, pretending to be attentive but unable to hide a healthy person's instinctive fear.

"They're holding me here. They beat me. They beat me very badly." Marianna raised her hand, showing an old yellow bruise; she had recently bumped into the corner of the wardrobe, and her body, tired, poisoned by her own blood, was slowly trying to heal itself.

"Beat me," she said once more confidently, too confidently, with the certainty of madness. And lightly, more softly, she pressed on, "Fascists. But you are our people, aren't you? Will you take me away?"

The electoral representatives hurried away. And Zhanna, for the only time in her mother's entire illness, was seized with pure, uplifting rage. What had they, the creatures who had invaded from the East, who had brought their damn referendums, done to her mother, her clear, bright, amazing mother?

Zhanna sensed that her mother was dying as a creator whose creation was crushed by evil, and she could not survive it. But what had she created? What? What?

She couldn't hold on to the peak of that liberating rage, collapsed back into the mess of her blackened feelings. Why had her mother turned against her and herself? Where had she gotten so much strength to agonize, to suffer, and to torment? Her strength should have been exhausted, allowing her to die. Why had she become a monster, devouring her daughter's life? What was there, deep inside her, that was still alive? Was it still her mother, or a new, terrible thing gripping Zhanna?

Zhanna threw back the blanket and got out of bed. The memories, the struggle of the two images of her mother in them, exhausted her to the point of nausea. In the bathroom, she leaned over the toilet and vomited bitter saliva, stomach juices, and it seemed to her that she was vomiting the poisoned days of her mother's illness, vomiting the heavy smell of feces and urine that lingered in the house.

She remembered, because her mother was often called to help at funerals, that nothing in the house could be touched, nothing could be disturbed. But she could no longer tolerate this musty air. And taking revenge on her mother, depriving her of the protection of the ritual, she began opening the windows, which Marianna had forbidden, and with difficulty she pushed out the stubborn latches, jammed since winter.

The July air, hot, with an intoxicating smell of flowers and herbs, poured in from the street. A dragonfly flew in, getting trapped in the curtains, and Zhanna suddenly recited what seemed to be dead, lost: "The dragonfly played all summer, and now it was winter." She was drawn into the distance, into the golden haze of the morning steppe on the dragonfly's trembling wings.

Suddenly light, she danced, whirled around the rooms, forgiving herself for the betrayal, blaspheming innocently. Her mother had turned away all the people she knew, forbidden them to enter the house, and now Zhanna was dancing the enforced loneliness out of her soul, the movements of the dance asking the world for help, so that it would notice her, send her salvation, comfort, extend a hand of support.

The doorbell rang.

Zhanna, still under the suggestive spell of the dance, still in the naive, desperate belief that her request could be heard, ran up and opened the door, forgetting that she was standing there in her nightie.

She recognized him.

It was Valka, Valet, her childhood sweetheart, the neighbor who had gone to Russia six years ago. Her mother had spoken of him only a couple of times since his departure, in passing, saying that he had gone to seek a better fortune, but Zhanna felt that he had left for a reason, and sometimes she remembered him, imagined what he was like there, what he had grown up to be like in Moscow, wondered why he did not come back, and imagined how he would look at her, grown up, if he came back . . .

So he was back. He came on his own, knocked on his own. Valetik, Valya, with reddish-blond hair. A neighbor, a man, a fool, a sweetheart.

VALET

Early in the morning, just before dawn, Valet was awakened by his cell phone.

"Valet? Headquarters now," the commander said and hung up.

The commander had never called him before. Only his deputies, local guys. Sort of like "militiamen." Valet knew them from childhood: they lived in the neighborhood. They worked in the paramilitary security of the mine, were involved in illegal sales of coal, and then opened a private agency, and he didn't consider them real officers.

He had thought when he first arrived that when he got to work, it would be like Uncle Georgy's regiment: platoon formation, training, orders . . . But it turned out to be almost like a gang: phone call, attack, do the job, and then scatter. At first it was very odd for him; Uncle Georgy had accustomed him to something else.

And those rallies outside the administration building . . . For the first time Valet found himself on the other side, among the protesters. No protective suit with plastic overlays, no helmet, no baton. A jacket, trousers, and a Russian flag in his hands. The Ukrainian cops formed a line opposite.

Cosmonauts like himself. In spacesuits and with shields, and a water cannon behind them. Valet wanted to join their ranks with his visor over his eyes, shoulder to shoulder! But he was supposed to play the civilian, shout slogans . . . He looked around, and locked eyes with two others from his regiment, whom Uncle Georgy had also sent on "vacation." The guys were miserable. They didn't feel comfortable on this side. Unaccustomed. It was like being naked. They wanted to go to the cops' side.

But Valet took a closer look at the police wall. With a knowing eye: how they kept formation, how they closed their shields, where their commanders were. He saw that the cops had no gusto, no spirit. They just stood there. If you pressed, if you pushed the crowd so that cobblestones and Molotov cocktails flew, they would give up, retreat, and their water cannon was just for show; they didn't know how to use it, they had chosen a stupid place for it, it would either hit their own people with the jet, or they would have to move it so that they could shoot from the flank.

It suddenly was ridiculous. He was used to standing on Moscow squares and avenues, near the Kremlin. And what was going on here? A tempest in a teapot. A sideshow. But he reprimanded himself: Uncle Georgy sent him, so bear with it. Uncle knew better. After all, how did Uncle get to Moscow? Through Chechnya. Through internal troops. He was promoted, made the right friends, showed and proved himself. Same here, Valet said to himself. If you prove yourself, you'll rise.

That's why he tried very hard to make himself known to the commander. The one whom Moscow had put in charge. Who held no post: just a man in civilian clothes, just a voice on the telephone. And now apparently, it was his chance.

Valet raced off. He drove his father's Zhiguli 9, bought back in Soviet times: a quarter of a century ago. But that was all right; it wasn't about the car. He's already got his eye on one: a black Volvo. He would have liked a BMW, of course, but that was incommensurate with his rank. There was this businessman who owned the Volvo: he had a gravel pit, his father-in-law worked in the prosecutor's office. There was no way he could have gotten close to it before, but now the word was that it was decided to take him down, to put him in the cellar, to take his business away, and Valet expected to be part of it—maybe he'd get lucky. They should have thrown him a piece a long time ago, he was a cadre, and Uncle Georgy was behind him.

As he drove the Zhiguli, he pictured putting Zhanna in the Volvo, wearing a white dress in the black car, and they would go to the Paradise, the militia pub, to celebrate their wedding, with champagne and shooting, everything as it should be.

He even felt affection for Marianna, who, it turns out, had both prepared Zhanna and died in time. Following a script. He had planned to make a move on Zhanna later, when she had recovered a little. But then he realized: he had to do it now, today, before she came to her senses; that's the best move, to come in as a neighbor, to help with the funeral. They knew him at the morgue, and he had a friend working at the cemetery where the fathers of Zhanna and Valet were buried.

"Oh, and we'll bury you, old Marianna," he thought complacently. "We'll build a hell of a monument to last forever. So that you will lie under it and never wake up."

Headquarters was a joke; they took over the sports center, posters still hung on the walls. He used to work out here himself as a kid. His father had put him in a boxing class. But it didn't work out. The coach said, "He doesn't have enough fighting spirit."

The commander, whom they knew only by his call sign, Monk, was sitting in his office, the former accounting office. He was unattractive, round-headed, with a reedy mustache, thin, smoky, and twitchy, as if devils were pounding on his joints with hammers. Valet, a big man, who had beefed up in the special regiment, where mass was needed to break up crowds, was afraid of him: Monk was spindly, but he had a frenzied temperament. There was a second man with him, in a mountain anorak, the kind everyone wore, but he could have had big letters on his forehead: he was military, a lieutenant or captain. Valet was sick of Monk, of playing partisan games.

"Where did you serve, Valya?" Monk asked.

"The Strategic Missile Forces," Valet reported.

The officer pressed his lips together.

"Don't you have any of our people?" he said.

"There are missiles there, and you have missiles, but smaller ones." Monk shrugged him off, making the officer pout. "Valya, we need to orient the boys on the ground. So come on, get on board, you're from here. And keep quiet afterward. They," Monk nodded his head at the officer, "are not here. And their car isn't here, either. So you understand."

"What's your last name, soldier?" asked the officer on the street.

"Call me Valet. I'm used to it," he replied, and he saw the displeasure he wanted to provoke on the officer's face.

However, the officer soon thawed out. Valet immediately guessed who he was: an air defense officer, the commander of the very SAM that had crawled down the street yesterday. The men had been smuggled here from Russia and left to their own devices; you had to be your own Susanin, leading yourself out of the woods in heroic fashion. And a SAM was not a shawarma stand; you had to hide it, especially if, as Monk said, this crew was not officially here.

Valet offered, "Let me take you around the town, show you places. And then you can decide where and how to go." And he took him straight to the closed mine, where there were a lot of secluded places and a lot of scrap metal. Not just a SAM—you could hide a cruiser and it wouldn't be visible from a satellite.

They passed the mine administration building. Broken windows, grass growing on the roof of the porch. There was a mosaic on the end of the building, a mosaic panel that covered all five floors. His father, when he was healthy, was very fond of explaining to him, a twerp, what it meant: miners rose from the bowels of the earth to break the shackles that bound the proletariat. The miners were huge, half naked, in rags of some kind, hammers in muscular hands, glares of rage on their red faces, and the people nicknamed the panel "They Didn't Get Paid."

But Valet's father used to swear when he heard that. He liked to say that the artist worked from life, and that he, a top worker, was called to the party committee to pose. Whether it was true or not, it always seemed to Valet that one of the giants did really have his father's features; after the mine collapse, he used to come here to be with his father of old.

But while Valet was in Moscow, and the mine was ownerless, the panel deteriorated, colored stones piling up under the wall. The miners lost a piece of a torso, an arm, a piece of a skull, and turned into sinister freaks, monsters, stubbornly climbing out of the underworld. Valet shuddered: the collapsing panel depicted exactly what had happened to his father. He used to take his father to the bathhouse—he liked the steam even when he was disabled—and saw the bodies of other old men, bent by underground labor, mangled by accidents, rock blows, and gas explosions, branded with the fading tattoos of Soviet times: like a living picture book, an atlas of a vanished world, an encyclopedia of symbols of its power and glory.

The antiaircraft gunner walked along, looking around closely, nodding his head approvingly. And Valet, following his gaze, sensed that the missile belonged here, among the abandoned mine buildings, the rusty skeletons of mining machines, as if it, the missile, had come to avenge the devastation here, the face of his father, mangled because of the pieces of mosaic that had fallen off: living and sentient metal that would hide among the dead metal.

In the army, he served at a silo of the Strategic Missile Forces, where a stupid, blunt-headed ballistic missile slept in the ground. This antiaircraft missile was much smaller, thinner, sharper. And the mines here were much deeper. But it was as if they were attracted to each other, antiaircraft missile and mine, mine and missile, like bullet and rifle barrel. And he suddenly sensed this mutual attraction as something real, as a physically tangible—in a rare moment—force of destiny.

"Let's go," said the officer. "Well done. Found a good place. Just what we need."

He led them back the other way, past the 3/4, past the spoiled shaft full of dead men.

His mother, when she sent him to Moscow, guessed where he had been, where he had been digging, where he had gotten dirty, why Marianna had made her statement. But she didn't ask any questions about blood that hadn't been washed. Valet convinced himself that he hadn't killed anyone. It was a ghost. Where else could a ghost be if not there? Marianna, the bloody witch, was mistaken. She had sent him away for nothing. But now that Marianna was gone, he was relieved to admit to himself: no, not a ghost. He could take a shovel and go and check it out. No one would care about an old murder now.

But there was something he was afraid of. Not even discovery, no. When he was a kid, the boys had whispered that some Coal Chomper lived in the abandoned mine works, that he dug passages under the village and could get into the basements. There also lived Good Shubin, an old man densely encased in wool who helped miners in trouble. Valet knew that it was just a childish fantasy, but could he have killed Shubin? The old miners said, after drinking a lot, that Shubin was gone, gone, gone.

After dropping off the rocket man and then turning into the courtyard of the house, he saw the neighbor's light curtains fluttering in the windows. Guessed what open windows meant and the chance it gave him.

When Zhanna opened the door, he sensed she was open, as well, to abandon, to foolish fearlessness, ready to be oblivious, to give herself up, to fall on his shoulder.

And by contrast, he remembered the dark autumn in Moscow. Alleyways blocked by police chains. Grid-fenced enclosures where people voluntarily went through metal detectors to a rally. A strange game in the streets and squares, and they, the special regiment, were the corrallers; it was their city, they could snatch anyone, anyone, out of the crowd, and no one would intercede, they would only take pictures on their phones, the herd, the sheep.

He had grabbed a very young girl who looked like Zhanna and dragged her toward the detention center, and the crowd parted. He shifted his hold on her; her clothes were pulled up, her belly and tits flashed. She had fear and shame in her eyes, yet right nearby, behind the bars, behind the chains, store windows were lit up, people were shopping.

If he dragged her aside, into a back alley, to expose her, the passersby would turn away, only speed up their pace, and that was all. He wanted to see this fear in Zhanna's eyes, but it was not yet time; he needed to wait, to relish: let her believe, let her trust him.

He thought that Zhanna would question him: where he had been, how he had lived. But Zhanna, having gotten dressed, behaved in the car like a doll, like a sleepwalker, and Valet again felt ironic gratitude to Marianna: she had died well; she had screwed up her daughter well! It was Zhanna's alienation that made him hold back, play the part of that childhood sweetheart, the unexpected helper and savior; he liked to prolong this state, her ignorance, her innocence.

True, at one moment she woke up: in the cemetery. Last fall, before his arrival, a thing had happened to the cemetery: the diggings had come too close, then the rains had washed up, and a good quarter of the cemetery land had crumbled into bits; the coal bed had subsided. The huge hole remained, with old monuments, coffins, crosses in it. There was no time to deal with it; there was a war, and how could you fix it, anyway? Zhanna's family grave was just on the edge; ten steps away and there was a precipice. Valet didn't know that; he never went to the cemetery. And Zhanna, it turns out, didn't know, either.

The gravediggers argued: "Fuck it, if you start digging, it will get worse, you'll land down there with the dead." And Zhanna came to the edge, looking perplexed, though she was a miner's daughter, and then she said, "I won't bury my mother here," and suddenly her gaze was clear and fresh, as if she, and not Valet, was in charge of things.

Well, he got it and answered politely, "It's only temporary. We'll rebury her later."

Suddenly like a switch was pressed, the doll was a doll again, as if the heat had made her woozy. And he gave a sign to the gravediggers: Dig, I'll take care of you. They got to it quickly; they must have realized who he was: Why the hell would they mess with militiamen? And Zhanna stood like a pillar while they dug. Valet then gave her a handful of earth to throw on the coffin, but she kneaded it, and it all slipped through her fingers. Valet got angry; she was too wooden. He wanted her to believe in his kindness with all her soul, so that she would be all the more bitter when he spoke to her differently.

But he took her home, wished her good evening, and promised to come back in the morning. And he went to the Paradise to commemorate, so to speak, and celebrate. Sashka Little was in there, Little because he wasn't small at all, a colleague, one of the men sent by Uncle Georgy. He and Sashka were from the same platoon, two rookies.

"Brother, hey." Sasha waved at him, hugging him tightly, in a brotherly way, and the bear hug brought back the memory of how the swollen crowd had crushed them in 2012 on Bolotnaya Square, and how they stood there, clasping their hands together in a special grip, holding the line. For a long time, the large body of the demonstration swayed and swelled, as if a whale were giving birth. But Valet, deafened by the clamor even in a helmet, though his muscles were already cramped from exertion, sensed that despite its size this crowd was still innocent. There was no beast in it. Flags were flying, skirmishes were boiling, but still the human mass would not get angry, would not rise in a single outburst, would not allow itself to be tamped down and trained. Someone wise and experienced in the operational headquarters was conducting, keeping hotheads from rushing things, from using gas and water cannons, letting the crowd boil, evaporate, and tire itself out.

Sashka was standing and hanging on the right: a Black man in plastic armor. He was lifted by the pressure of the crowd, and he looked like a cosmonaut, hovering in a pose possible only in weightlessness.

"If you don't want to be a miner, go be a cosmonaut," Valet's father used to tease, to prove that there was no future but the mine. And little Valya muttered, "I will be a cosmonaut." He dreamed of a rocket to fly far, far away.

There, at the rally, Valet broke through: he became a cosmonaut! A cosmonaut without a rocket. But actually: he lived at his uncle's house near the VDNKh Exhibition Center, where pavilions displayed national economic achievements, overlooking the stele emblazoned with the words "To the Conquerors of Space," a titanium rocket on a titanium plume rushing upward. He was a cosmonaut. He was the man in the helmet with the power. A ninja turtle, a superhero. And they were biomass. That's what Uncle Georgy used to say: biomass.

Sashka poured, Valet drank. And remembered how he went to the square the next day, while the others were sleeping it off in the barracks. Why? He did not know.

The square and the adjoining streets were empty, just as riverbeds and streams are empty when the floods subside. The crowd that had squeezed through the bottlenecks of the surrounding streets, embankments, bridges, and cordons yesterday had left behind these traces of flow and pressure: garbage, trampled leaflets and white ribbons, broken branches in the public garden, furrows in the paths: some had walked, others were dragged. He took a new look at the square trapped between the river and the canal, remembered yesterday's human mincemeat, forced to compact, to fit into these narrows. He had never seen so many people together before.

Like the mine, he thought.

The mine, that Shaft 3/4, had suddenly become something akin to a measure for bulk goods, for grits. Once you know about it, you measure everything against it: Would these fit?

A forgotten word problem from school popped into his head, something about density and volume.

A crowd spread out over a square.

A crowd crammed into a mine shaft.

He lit a cigarette, saw bloodstains on the sand, saliva, and a shiny gold tooth.

"They knocked it out," he thought lazily. "It could have been one of them, with a branch, an elbow."

The tooth hypnotized him. Valet bent down, picked it up, wiped the blood and sand off on his pant leg.

A crown.

He didn't keep it. Tossed it in the canal.

He sensed that yesterday was only the beginning. There'd be another day when they'd be given the command to really knead the crowd. Knead it with clubs, like rolling pins, so that the bloody juice would come out, so that the human dough would rise and be ready for the molds.

That night, when he came home drunk and sat on the porch to smoke his last cigarette, his feet almost carried him to Zhanna, to her dark windows.

To block the urge, he looked up into the sky, found the firefly of a satellite flying in the darkness, and burst into a hiccupping, earthly laugh.

"I'm a cosmonaut! *Whoo!* Let's go!"

THE GENERAL

General Korol started work early in the morning in the old building of the KGB—later taken over by the SBU—in his old office on the second floor with a view of the slag heap, which sometimes spontaneously started burning, giving off gray ashy clouds like a volcano. The old walls painted a nauseating green were now paneled in fake wood. The windows were plastic, new. And there was a new dropped ceiling. But the safe for secret documents was the same, as was the three-pronged key; they had just changed the inventory number.

He should have been going through the surviving files of Ukrainian agents: his assistants had selected the most important ones. But he quickly got bored. They weren't going anywhere, the agents. And why bother looking? He could tell without any documents who, most likely, had been recruited by the SBU. It was a district center, not the capital. The posts and positions of operational interest were not infinite. Especially now that the mine was shut down. He wrote the plan of its operational service himself when he was a major. And the plan was in effect until the mine closed; the SBU did not change it. He wrote it here, in this office. There had been a cactus on the windowsill, a gray prickly dwarf: an inheritance from Major Anikin, who occupied this office before him.

Anikin. Anika the warrior, they called him behind his back. How old was he in 1978 when the young Korol was attached to him? Too much trouble to do the math. Over fifty, for sure. He was an alcoholic, Major Anikin. He was even stripped of his lieutenant-colonel rank once. Reprimand upon reprimand. And he was a bad operative, recruiting without fire, just to fulfill the recruitment plan. Then Korol inherited his agents: one never turned up, another just repeated rumors, the third one was always sick, complaining about his health, a wimp.

Korol thought they kept Anikin out of pity. He was listed as personnel at the mine on the level of janitor or guard, but of course was neither. Anikin rose to the rank of major, but had no higher education; he still confused a caisson with a casserole, thick head like cast-iron.

But Korol, a young blood, Andropov's boy, was of a different mold: he had graduated from a mining technical school in Russia, in Kursk, and had managed to work for a couple of years in the Kursk Magnetic Anomaly, in iron ore quarries, where open-pit mining was practiced, before he was unexpectedly invited to come to the first department of the production association.

He thought that they would scold him about secret documents, because in the evening he had failed to return drawings that required clearance, he was delayed and worked with them at night. A man in a gray jacket, his eyeglasses flashing, said sternly, "We are offering you honorable work." And he, silly kid, at first hesitated; he didn't want to get into the yoke. He blurted, "Mining ore is also honorable." And the committee's messenger calmly told him, "The party knows better where you should work. The party committee recommended you, and that's it." He was unmarried, his grandfather was missing in action in the war, and his father was married to a priest's granddaughter. But apparently, they needed smart personnel who knew mining, so they turned a blind eye to his deficits.

He finished his studies and was assigned to the Donbas, as a deputy to Major Anikin, who was engaged in operational maintenance of the Marat mine, and who was to retire in a year. To be his successor. He expected that the new coworkers would not take kindly to him; the position seemed to be promising, but he quickly noticed that no one was rushing to be Anikin's heir. When the major came out of the hospital, he brought him up to speed and told him about Shaft 3/4.

When Korol heard it, he didn't believe it. He didn't understand how such a thing could happen. He wanted, like a fool, like Doubting Thomas, to see, to make sure. Anikin smirked and drove him there. A pile of coal slag, and under it a concrete plug. Enjoy the view.

He couldn't sleep that night. A strange, almost anti-Soviet thought crossed his mind: Why do the people up there in the Central Committee of the party need so many dead Jews? Why do they keep them, like a miserly old woman with pennies in a jar? Like the gold reserves in the basement of the state bank? Like packets of a hundred bills? For what?

To bring out the treasure one day at the politically opportune moment, to lay out several thousand in front of Willy Brandt or Helmut Schmidt and say, Take it, don't be shy, it's all yours, and we have more?

So as not to indulge the Zionists, who would use this example of Jewish victimhood? Not give them additional trump cards?

And every answer seemed to fit.

But the longer the sleepless night lasted, the deeper he thought, the clearer he realized that there was no real answer. It was a mystery. After all, calling things by their proper names meant that the Soviet regime, which defeated fascist Germany, was covering up the fascist crime. Literally. They should be shoving these bodies, these dead people, in the face of the West: see what they are really like, your Chancellor Kiesinger, your Germans, your hatchlings!

But no, they didn't do that. They kept them. They protected them as their own property.

After all, what had Anikin told him: in addition to operational maintenance of the active Marat mine, Shaft 3/4 was also operationally maintained. The coffer of the dead. To keep people from asking questions: What's in there? To make those who knew keep silent. Occasionally a commission of specialists from Moscow came to check on its condition.

Of course, he had been taught about nationalistic tendencies, about the special danger of Zionism. Babyn Yar in

THE LADY OF THE MINE

Kyiv was cited as an example: there, they said, unstable elements gathered at the place of execution of peaceful Soviet citizens, propagating lies about the oppression of Jews in the Soviet Union.

But, he thought, there were no dead Jews in Babyn Yar itself. They were burned, then the remains were ground to dust by special machines. But here . . . Coal. A mine. No air.

They were in there.

Preserved like canned goods. Was it humane to leave them there? It wasn't the only mine like that. In other places in the area, Jews were executed and thrown into mine shafts. But there were memorials, plaques, again, not to Jews, of course, but to the memory of Soviet citizens, to the memory of miners, and the committee made sure that Zionists did not use this for their own purposes.

Then why not raise them? Why not rebury them? Because it would make too big a cemetery?

It was a long night. He was a Soviet man. Righteous. He'd lost his father in the war. That's what made it hard to understand, to accept: Why weren't we investigating? Why were we covering up the Nazis' crime? A whole fucking mine, thousands and thousands. We were still hunting down German accomplices, the punishers, now old men. The Investigation Department was doing its best, working on archival materials. The ones they found were tried by the people's court. We exhumed the victims, reburied them solemnly. We informed the public in the newspapers: here it is, the vicious grin of fascism! We made movies like *No Statute of Limitations*. But here was the crime of the century, of unimaginable scale, and, most importantly, with clear evidence.

Now the general's desk was covered by the volumes of the secret file, which the district department had kept on the mine since 1921. Cardboard folders of three hundred pages. OGPU, NKVD, MGB, KGB . . . Forty-nine volumes. Their yellowed pages were like thin layers of oil shale. Year after year, decade after decade. He had compiled them from 1978 to 1991.

A time machine. The eighties, seventies—all neat, documents typed by typists. Routine, regime and secrecy checks, emergency investigations, planned recruitment of agents, preventive measures. The language was clerical, verbose, and the subordinate clauses grew and multiplied. The sixties, fifties: half the papers were handwritten, and the language was different, dim-witted, with wild mistakes, written by Stalin's people, who were finishing out their service, finishing out their lives.

But before the war, in the thirties . . . Twenty-three volumes in one decade. Rarely, occasionally a typewritten document, most by hand, drunken handwriting, illegible, lines skipping. And the volumes seemed thicker, though the number of pages was exactly the same, the standard size. It was like going down into a huge cellar. To the blood-soaked coal age. There were diagrams on paperboard made with a drafting pen, red and blue ink, in those volumes.

Diagrams of cases that were conducted in the mine.

A diagram of the Polish conspiracy. A diagram of Trotskyist nests. A diagram of the Ukrainian national underground.

A diagram of a sabotage organization of "specialist" workers. A diagram of a fascist center. A diagram of the White
Guard Union.

Diagrams. Diagrams. Diagrams.

That was why the volumes were so bloated.

Levels. Circles. Arrows.

Each one looked like a blueprint crosssection of the mine.
Or the plan of its administrative structure. The Chekists
extracted these fictitious conspiracies from the mine.
Confessions were extracted, a mountain of them. Execution
sentences. The target goals were met and exceeded.

Anikin brought this file to his office, read it. He read it
and understood then why it was impossible to exhume Jews
from Shaft 3/4. He understood and became a different man.

The future General Korol.

You couldn't, because they couldn't be extracted separately. Once you started uncovering, unscrewing, digging, the entire past would emerge. Both German and our
own, Soviet. That's how it was in the mine, mixed, inter-
twined. And not only in the mine. In life. And that's why, as
Lermontov wrote, "A heavy stone lay on him, so he could not
rise from his coffin."

I pity you, comrade Jews. But what can one do?

He realized it in 1978, on the morning of the seventh
of July, almost exactly thirty-six years ago. And he realized
something else that not all the Chekists realized. He was
a miner, a special kind of man. Miners have a developed
sixth sense, a trained intuition, like military radar. They go

underground, they know death; the farther from heaven, the closer to hell.

He realized that the Soviet regime's real power was revealed by its willingness to cover up the enemy's guilt and evil. Only the strongest of the strong, who was above simple morality, could do that. He would serve the regime faithfully, for he now knew its truth: it was easy to kill strangers, harder to kill one's own, but to dare to cover up the enemy's sin required great wisdom and unlimited might.

He reread the file, comparing his faith and devotion to what had happened afterward: perestroika, the fall of the Soviet Union, his departure for Russia. Was that revelation false? After all, the Union didn't stand. And the Committee did not save it. There were too few of us, he answered himself. Few who understood the truth. Who took communion. Our power did not reside even in the Lubyanka. Not in Iron Felix. But in this mine, in Shaft 3/4.

He realized that he did not care at all about what was happening at the front, about the affairs of the war, about the failure of this, as it was, "Russian Spring," invented out of whole cloth by his junior colleagues: only a few cities were captured, but the expectations were huge!

But it was back. The mine. An underground scepter of power, ten times bigger than the Alexander Column. For decades it had waited, untouched, uncorked, as if the seals placed on it held a formidable power. Here, he thought with a flash of joy, the Soviet Union had never gone away. It endured like a spell.

The word *spell* brought back another memory. This case was not in the local archives; it had been taken to Russia, but the general remembered the file's cover perfectly well: "Werewolf." They were looking for a defector, an army junior lieutenant who had been captured in 1941 and joined the Germans, the punishers. He brutalized without restraint. They searched for almost four decades, in six regions, made duplicate cases, agents tried his family, and they caught three others who accidentally fell into the net.

The man, it turned out, was always in plain sight. Close by. When a witness identified him from a newspaper photo, they didn't believe her at first: Why are you casting aspersions on a respected man? He was the director of a collective farm, a leader, his chest covered with ribbons and badges. As Soviet as you could be. He didn't leave with the Germans. He hid out in the woods. He managed to change his documents in 1944, enlisted in the Red Army under a false name, reached Berlin, received awards. Member of the party, member of the bureau of the district committee. Member of the veterans' council. *Ha-ha.*

Korol, in charge of the case, was learning to read people: he felt in his gut that the man's former beastly nature was real. He wasn't only acting on German orders. And this new Soviet man was also real.

Reincarnated.

And the punisher, knowing that he would be sentenced to death, stalled for time. He gave away his accomplices one by one. And then he promised to take them to the grave of

SERGEI LEBEDEV

executed partisans. He did: to an abandoned clay pit, over-grown with grass. The soldiers shoveled; the investigator gave the prisoner a cigarette. Soon the bodies could be seen. Clay is a good preservative. The prisoner finished his cigarette. He grinned at the sun.

Suddenly the investigator, the experienced old man Polivanov, shouted, "Stop it, stop!" waving his hands at the soldiers.

The grave was ours, a Soviet grave. Arrested men whom the NKVD shot during the retreat. Polivanov immediately understood from the manner of execution. The Germans had a different way of doing things.

The prisoner was laughing hard and coughing terribly; his throat hadn't been scorched by tobacco for a long time. The soldiers were embarrassed, couldn't understand why the investigator was chasing them away from the grave.

. . . Anikin, by the way, when he turned over his caseload, said straightforwardly, "There is something strange here, that materialism cannot explain yet." Korol, though a mining man, dismissed it.

Then he began to notice: yes, there was. Something you couldn't catch or recruit. Someone else would have paid no attention, but he was no country bumpkin; he had grown up in the mines, reading and listening to stone. There weren't any cheap tricks, no knocking and scraping that miners tell stories about. Only a strange feeling, on the verge of percep-tion, of a presence.

That was when he began to look closely, not reporting to

anyone—they'd send him to the nuthouse. He listened to the stories of the agents, to the rumors in the city. He used the methods his predecessors in western Ukraine had employed to identify the Bandera fighters in their lairs, by connections, by the thin threads that stretched from them into ordinary grounded life, where people baked bread, made moonshine, mended and washed laundry.

That's how he spotted Marianna, "Snow White," the laundry manager. Strange things were said about her. And strange things had to be connected.

He made a case against her. But he couldn't prove anything. And he grew fiercer, sensing that there was a tie between her and Shaft 3/4. But something protected her, like the cloak of invisibility that warded off people's gazes. That enflamed him: All the committee's X-ray apparatus, all the surveillance and wiretaps for nothing? No, no, you cheat! You won't get away!

It was almost love, almost passion: he wanted so much to expose her, to make her his prisoner, to find out her secret: What was hiding there in the mine? Who or what was he, the one Korol called Engineer? Of course, it was passion, of course! His superiors hinted that it was time to get married, a KGB officer should be a family man; for his career it was a plus, albeit a small one. Many women were interested in him, tried to catch him, but he had only Marianna on his mind, as strange as an alien and painfully desirable: because of her secrets, which Soviet people were not supposed to have, and because of her purity, insulting and creating a desire to possess her, break her, make her like everyone else.

Tomorrow, the general said to himself.

Tomorrow.

Tomorrow Semyon would bring her.

It was time.

THE ENGINEER

I am the shaft.

The tree of three worlds connecting depth, surface, and sky.

I created it, designed it, dreaming of making people happy, of ushering in an age of prosperity when the earth would bestow its riches on everyone. It was the Tower of Babel in reverse—tipped deep into the earth, its aim was the earth, not the sky.

The 3/4 shaft, designed to extract coal, was its core. The deepest on the continent, reaching the richest seams. The widest, allowing the pace of extraction to soar.

I still exist, because I put my soul into the mine, dreaming on a Babylonian scale, the unprecedented depth, the complexity of construction, and its prophetic meaning: more of the earth's black bread—more steel, more useful machines, more freedom for mankind. The socialists wanted only to take away and divide, but I wanted to prove that the riches of the earth were enough for everyone, and the main issue was the technical underdevelopment of the productive forces, the narrowness of capitalist thinking. I also invested the capital inherited from my father, becoming a co-owner for the first time and securing the right to insist on my engineering solutions. Mines were named after things in those days—where they were, who owned them. I named mine Sophia: wisdom.

With machines of my design we went through the 3/4 shaft in fifteen months. There was dirt and poverty all around; miners of other joint-stock companies lived in dugouts, received water only for drinking. They remembered the bloody work of Cossack sabers and spades during the recent cholera riot. They remembered how the soldiers beat the rebels to death, with the military doctors measuring the blows to deem who could take how much. How the government troops distributed weapons to the peasants and set them against the workers. And I, contrary to reality, dreamed of a mine of universal abundance, and at last it was possible to start mining.

But that was 1905. The first revolution. And the Socialist Revolutionary strike committee of the basin called for a strike. Oh, I knew that at other mines agitators had long been active. Party cells had been set up: the coal works, you might say, were a natural place for underground activity, for hide-and-seek with the police. There was dynamite, and where there was dynamite, there were also bombings. But I was sure that my mine, my Sophia, would not be affected by this revolutionary contagion. We paid well, and the workers liked a mine designed to make their labor easier.

And I would have held on to my miners. But I was in Germany, placing an order in a pump factory. By the time

105

I was able to return, when train traffic was restored, it was too late. The police and Cossacks opened fire on the rally at Shaft 3/4: twenty-seven dead. I think it was a provocation of competitors who wanted to disrupt our success, ruin our reputation forever, intimidate us. Otherwise, it was impossible to explain why the bodies were dumped into Shaft 3/4 on someone's command. The investigation never established who gave the order, police or Cossacks.

Of course, they were retrieved later. But it was too late.

Blood had been spilled. In the long fall of bodies to the bottom of the shaft, a pattern emerged, a motif of evil that then repeated itself a hundredfold. Shaft 3/4 was cursed.

When we put it into service, it turned out that its added width was its Achilles' heel. It crumbled too easily; it was vulnerable to tectonic movement, to shock waves from coal mining explosions. We mothballed it and laid a second mining shaft: a standard, narrow shaft. I tried to figure out how to save the old shaft, and I found a solution, but the First World War started. I was German; I could have left. But I couldn't leave her, Sophia. I was granted citizenship, changed my name to something more Russian. I had not yet given up hope of correcting the mistake and reviving the dead shaft, which was the only one that could bring an outstanding, supernatural result. I treated it as a cause for good, as a creation of the future, which would need my help to become reality.

But what had I really created?

I found out when the Civil War broke out.

That first, ill-fated firing squad, those twenty-seven bodies dumped in the shaft seemed to have paved the way for future evil, providing a hint about where to hide corpses.

Armies, troops, detachments, gangs came and went, lingering sometimes for a month, sometimes for a day. They plundered. Forcibly mobilized people into their ranks. Fleeing miners who did not want to work without pay, without food rations, were flogged en masse. But the military doctor no longer counted the blows. They arrested. They executed. And everyone knew where the previous victims had been killed and where to take the prisoners.

Don Cossacks shot members of the miners' councils. Red partisans shot Cossacks. White Guards, Reds. German occupation troops, partisans. Makhnovists, Denikins. Reds shot Germans and Makhnovists. Tortured. Poked out their eyes. Cut throats. Perpetuum mobile, a tautology of violence.

And all the bodies were placed in Shaft 3/4, six hundred meters deep. I created a biblical treasure trove of the abyss. And I fooled myself for too long.

I could have fled; I could have gone with my retreating compatriots, with the Germans. But once again I could not make up my mind to leave her, my creation, my wife, my Sophia . . . When the Reds finally took power, I wanted to believe that the Soviets would give me the opportunity to restore the mine that had been damaged during the fighting and, most importantly, to clean up the corpses, to repair, to start up Shaft 3/4. The surviving miners wrote a letter of recommendation: "Always actively sympathized with the labor movement." I saw that my dream of the mine as a cornucopia, of a human culture of labor was close to the dreams of the communists. Hoping to retain my authority, I offered them my services.

Commissar Martyshenko, a Baltic sailor, a stoker—that was why they put him in charge of the coal region—listened to me briefly and answered, looking at me with a single eye twitching because of his contusion.

"You will be the director! Go ahead! But let's name the mine in the Soviet way: Marat's name! In honor of the heroic battleship *Marat* that strangled the 1919 counterrevolution in Kronstadt."

I wanted to say that this was wrong, that a name is given only once, but suddenly I recognized the commissar's right: I had wanted to create Sophia, and yet what I had created was worthy to bear the name of a Jacobin who opened the way to fratricide and was killed by a dagger.

The commissioner would not permit restoring Shaft 3/4 and removing the bodies: let it be like a mass grave. And I convinced myself that as the Bolsheviks would settle down, that men like Martyshenko would be replaced by people who understood and would support my projects. We just had to wait. Give them the coal they demanded.

I rebuilt the mine. Started production. I wrote a forward-looking development project. I was waiting for praise and awards. But I was removed from my position, which Martyshenko took for himself, and made merely an engineer. One of many. I was a "specialist," an alien class element, a relic of the previous era. They didn't need my imaginary ideal mine, a technological miracle requiring advanced machinery and the highest quality labor. All they needed was coal.

The Shakhty Trial of 1928, arrests of old bourgeois mining specialists, bypassed me. I began to think that I could not be arrested. I didn't contact the former owners living abroad. The workers would not claim that I was cruel in prerevolutionary times, on the contrary. What was there to fear?

But I was afraid. I saw icons that had been confiscated from the peasants burned in the market squares. I saw my colleagues who had gone to serve the Soviets and were given everything, ate their fill, turning into overseers.

And the mine, with the name change, seemed to have changed its character. It became capricious, fraught: a carriage goes off the rails, then a collapse, then a gas explosion, then a pump fails . . . An immediate investigation: Was it sabotage? Martyshenko fumed, Martyshenko demanded punishment, but how could the mine be punished?

I was there to see the worst: the famine in the winter of 1933. Dying men roamed the village streets: peasants fleeing from the collective farms that were left without grain. Moscow demanded coal, Moscow thundered and rained dispatches, but production was falling; miners were dying, too, and some managed to get through the cordons to escape, and in January the police arrested the first cannibal in a nearby village. Bodies were not buried: the police dumped them in 3/4, saving their strength.

When I was arrested, accused of sabotaging the plan, I even thought I deserved it. During interrogations, seeking testimony, the investigator Krasov showed me a fictitious diagram of sabotage connections, resembling the blueprint of the mine: branched, divided into levels. In fact, it was also a mine. Its paper twin, a well of torment.

They were no longer executing people at Shaft 3/4. But even the dead executed in prison or lost in the camps went to the mine's total credit, to its fatal balance.

I was sentenced to five years. In the Ural camp I worked as a mining engineer. Like Jonah inside the whale, I was there through the most dangerous, deadly years. I stayed there when my term was up, enlisted as a volunteer worker. And in 1939, a courier from the NKVD brought a paper: return to the mine. They had overdone it. They had killed almost everyone who could ensure production. Including Martyshenko.

I dreamed of Sophia in the camp, when all other dreams had disappeared. Majestic and rational, she was like a desecrated temple, a tainted creation crying for help: mangled, distorted, the only visible evidence of my genius, and I was tied to her by an invisible thread, for I realized that there would be no second chance, no second Sophia.

Then came the war. Germany was rapidly advancing. I will not lie: I held out hope that the Germans, former compatriots, would behave reasonably, would understand the potential of my plans to rebuild the mine, or at least would not interfere. And I would give them coal, buy them off, as I bought off the Bolsheviks.

Retreating, the Soviets shot everyone in the prison; the bodies were dumped into Shaft 3/4: it was always handy when the killers were in a hurry. The mine was set to explode. But the men who'd been ordered to unblock the firing pin of the detonation device had fled. And if they had stayed and tried to set the explosion, there would be only a fizzle: the remaining miners had disconnected the wires of the device.

The Germans had already been here twenty years ago. The appointment was made wisely: Lieutenant Klopp, who then commanded a platoon guarding the mine, had risen through the ranks and now commanded a battalion of rear troops. The combat units soon left for the east, and Klopp summoned me, appointed me director, and demanded that I urgently restore production.

I obeyed.

I had always obeyed.

All I asked was that I be given Soviet prisoners of war from a camp nearby: a ready workforce. But Klopp refused: it was out of his hands. The POWs were being starved to death. As for the bodies, Klopp also knew where to put them.

He didn't care that I was a Jew. Coal has no nationality. But then the others came. Special units under special command. They occupied a wing in the former NKVD department, where the investigator Krasov (shot by his own people while I was in the camp) had once laid out before me the blueprints of a fictitious underground.

In the spring they ordered all the Jews to gather at the station. I knew there were many of our tribe in the town. It was on the very edge of the Pale of Settlement line, after all. But I never realized how many. The sheer number—the station was thronged with people—made the thought of killing us ridiculous.

Even when we were driven to the mine, I thought we were being led to the works. I walked inside the crowd, and I was safe in their numbers, protected by the cardinal inequality of those leading and the led. I think they, too, felt this effect of the giant crowd, numb and yet alive in the simple physiological sensation of magnitude, the way a herd of ungulates in the savannah probably feels its invulnerability as a species.

But if I had thought then as a paleontologist—the only kind of scientist who knows the true, absolute catastrophes of existence, sweeping away thousands of species, scraping the biosphere—what would it have changed?

I am coal.

I am slowly transforming.

Coal was the substance of power, giving birth to metal to make rails and cannons, to build the locomotive that would carry them pulled by the power of burning coal.

Coal was the flesh of prehistory, the dead organics, the ashes of bygone eras. Coal was the fuel of death, the integral element of violence; I wanted to create a cornucopia, but I opened Pandora's box. Coal, burning in the furnaces, made it possible to advance, to conquer, to arrest, to take away in echelons, to cut space, to destroy states. Coal fueled war, coal fueled the extermination of men, and now I am coal myself.

Oh, this love of dictatorships for miners, for the special caste that extracted the substance of power, dangerous because of the accompanying methane, as if charged with death. This love was deeper and greater than economic causality: in it, the dictator recognized and affirmed the naturalness of power, its involvement in the circulation of the animate and inanimate, its connection to the reptilian world of prehistory, which originated in the swamps of the Carboniferous period and left us the reptilian brain, the oldest part of us, the motor of the struggle for survival that dominates the mind of the dictator himself.

We who have become coal were also the substance of power. Only not the literal one that moved armies and echelons. We embodied power over the posthumous, an afterlife like that of the ancient deities. Some, the brown ones, executed us, and others, the red ones, corked us forever, like a genie in a bottle.

They were fierce, deadly enemies. But their secret affinity, their kinship, was hidden in us, in our posthumous rejection. The law would say these were two different crimes—murder and covering up murder—but if an enemy covered up for an enemy, who were they really to each other?

When the Soviets came back, they opened up Shaft 3/4 into which bodies had been hastily dumped by the Germans. They removed blocks of coal, pieces of equipment. Got to the top layer of bodies covered in caustic. Exhumed a few bodies. And then they sealed us up again. Filled the mouth with a concrete plug. The work lasted two weeks.

It was during those two weeks that I realized you have no idea how many spirits inhabit your netherworld. But the vast majority of them are, by human standards, unconscious or mindless. Contrary to your fanciful books, they can neither remember nor suffer. They thrash about longing and sullen, exhausting themselves and dissolving. I, too, was like that: I was prevented from disappearing only by the mine I had created, which posthumously gave me what I had put into it during my lifetime: the wasted heat of talent.

When the Soviet soldiers dug us out, I woke up with just a glimmer of light in the darkness. But this glimmer made it possible to realize that we had been found, we would soon be extracted, our petrified bodies would be separated, and we would be consigned to the earth in dignity. My agonizing, feral, absurd, captive existence would finally end.

I was galvanized and awakened by the hope of deliverance. When they began installing structures in the neck of the shaft, I first thought it was for the winches that would lift us up. And even when I saw that it was a mold for a concrete plug, I didn't believe it.

Why? Why leave us here? Why?

My current existence is but a lingering stunned amazement, a long echo of that "Why?" Although I know the answer.

A murderer can denounce a murderer. A villain can hypocritically rebuke a villain. Cast accusations, bring witnesses, open old graves, thereby whitewashing himself, clothed in the garb of goodness, pretending to be a doer of justice.

It would seem that this was what should have been done to us. To organize the trial of the century, the trial of Nazism, the reverse hecatomb, the fiercest denunciation possible.

But we were left underground. Was it the secret kinship of ideologies? The solidarity of criminals?

The Germans, finding Poles executed by Soviets at Katyn, spread the word. The Soviets, when they found us, were silent.

The Germans plunged us into darkness because they did not want to see us in this world. The Soviets didn't bring us into the light because they couldn't accept us, count us as victims. Didn't want to see us dead. Couldn't allow the primacy of suffering to belong to the Jews. And they could not uncork the vessel because below us lay the Reds killed by the Reds; if you take us out, you will have to take them out, too.

In this simplicity of explanation, in the ease with which the evil of murder is multiplied by the evil of its concealment, lies the overlap, the hitch of complicity.

The point of convergence.

The point of coincidence.

We were handled by the special division of the Tenth Archive Department, which kept the sites of secret Soviet executions on a balance sheet: checked on the continuing secrecy, built departmental vacation homes and sports centers over mass graves, planted, if necessary, a forest, prevented the subsidence of the soil . . . But we, locked in the mine, were terra incognita: nobody knew what was happening to us. Trusted persons from specialized research institutes discussed underground processes: Decay? Corruption? Would the released gases blow off the concrete cork? Would the groundwater undo the petrification? What chemical solutions should be used, then? What diameter wells should be drilled to inject them?

And we, we turned to stone.

DAY THREE

ZHANNA

Zhanna slept.

"If anything happens to me, you'll have a dream," her mother told her as she walked her to the institute, as if joking. "You will recognize it."

Zhanna understood these words this way: If something bad happened to her mother, she, Zhanna, would receive a message in a dream. She believed it. She waited. And then, when Marianna fell ill, and the dream had not come in advance, did not warn her, she was disappointed and dismissed it: empty words.

But now Zhanna, who had been sleepwalking through the day, who had buried her mother numbly, woke up at night, in the dream's unearthly manifestation. It flowed through her mind like a river, on whose mirrorlike surface, illuminated by the moon's silver light, the visions of the past played out: unrecognized before, but now made discernible as milestones, signs of destiny.

A late child, she had been born to her mother seemingly on her own, for Marianna had no plans for parenthood, no eagerness to conceive. A late child, as if her mother had calculated to send her as far into the future as possible.

Her personal future was always uncertain. Her mother didn't rush her, didn't obligate her. She did not drag her to clubs and groups to nurture her early talent. She did not demand good grades: go to school, study, and that was fine. Appearing apathetic and without aspirations, Zhanna had actually realized that she, the daughter of her mother, was expected to have a long period of maturation. But illness, death, and war had taken them both by surprise, thrown them out of a gradual growing up.

A girl. A virgin. And that didn't bother her, didn't impel her. Zhanna recalled in her dream how she would look at her mother and think involuntarily, Had she really made love with my father, body to body, and been pregnant with me? Marianna sometimes seemed so unfamily-oriented, so unfemale that Zhanna felt sorry for the dead father, whom she did not know. And at the same time Zhanna felt that even if the father were alive, they would still be two: mother and daughter.

That was how it had to be.

Unattractive, quiet—so that others would not look at her, would not be interested. Pale: part nun, part mermaid. Blood of the West and blood of the East in a strange mixture, as if they dampened each other's ardor.

Colorless. Not fond of bright things, as if it was physically difficult for her to bear the presence of saturated colors: carmine, azure, purple. Never getting tan in the southern sun. Neither did Marianna.

When her mother became ill and sank into oblivion during the day, the whole house was left at Zhanna's complete disposal for the first time in her life. All its nooks and crannies and hiding places. Like a thief, she searched the shelves and cupboards: she was looking for the family history, realizing how little she knew about the past, about her ancestors.

The ignorance of earlier familial history, overshadowed by her mother's existence, suddenly became blatant, gaping. But she found nothing, no photos, except for two or three dozen familiar ones, no documents, no diaries. No surprise about her father; he was from the orphanage, grew up on his own, and came here to the mine on assignment. His kin died in that old war. But mother and grandmother? It was as if they came out of nowhere. They lived among people, but not with people, choosing spouses without kin and tribe, without a hometown. She felt a sharp, hopeless loneliness in that anonymity.

And now in the dream, the feeling of being a laggard bird went away, replaced by a sense of belonging. The dream, like water, flowed through her, enlightening her inner vision, cleansing her body and soul. And Zhanna recognized through time and distance special women who were removed, hidden from ordinary life: not witches, not sorceresses, not healers, not herbalists—the White Ladies, who walk the earth unrecognized.

Wanderers wherever they were, but no one could say exactly where their roots were: their traces lost, their biographies cut off. Men took them young from their families, married them, took them to distant lands, kidnapped them, cutting off ties of their lineage. But the men didn't matter: they only thought they had power.

These women matured late, but they did not grow old for a long time, being part of that power of renewal that was embedded in time. Not the greatest beauties. Not born housewives. Local and foreign. Obedient to the call of a hidden destiny. They could live, exist, accumulate goods, earn a good name—and suddenly disappear into the night, melt away like fog. And the memory of them faded at the same speed as they settled in the new land.

No healing. No fortune-telling. They didn't cure cattle. They didn't gather secret herbs. They didn't make potions. They didn't attract men or lure them away. They didn't divine the future. They didn't preach. They didn't take female apprentices. But they cleaned, washed, laundered. They did not let places and people become dirty. They worked with water, near water, as laundresses and aides. They boiled bandages and linen, washed blood and sweat; they died, perished, almost disappeared in the cruel wars, in the evil of the past century. A secret sisterhood.

In her dream, Zhanna saw them visiting her mother when her father was away on business trips, to renew the bond, to check their sister's spirit, to support her if necessary. She remembered how in her childhood she would wake up in the morning feeling that someone had been in the house, who left no gift, no candy, only a familiar smell of cleanliness and comfort, slightly different from her mother's, a fragrance with a touch of lavender. Now in her dream, she understood that they had been in her room while she slept, looking at her, mentally encouraging her,

touching her forehead with their hands, guarding her, blessing her, and this secret inspiration was speaking, revealing
itself in her now.

She understood why both her mother and grandmother
loved to dance, to be the soul of dance. The rhythm and
rotation revealed the generous essence of the gift, joining
labor and fun, giving birth to a chain of special moments to
ward off evil. She recognized their charms, pure, weightless,
transparent, natural, not knowing the dark, inflamed strain
of magic. She accepted anew the poverty of their life, the
paucity of amusements that bothered her father, who as if by
chance lost the craving for smoking and drinking. She realized why her mother never venerated the war, did not bring
flowers to war memorials, did not celebrate Victory Day, did
not honor the memory of the Soviet soldiers.

As she soared above the town in her dreams, she recognized with new senses why her mother was here. She saw the
drama imprinted in the landscape.

She felt the fatal division of the border, the forces of the
states, Ukraine and Russia, colliding on the West-East axis:
the axis on which their house stood with Zhanna's windows
facing the sunset, the neighbors' windows facing the sunrise.

She watched the same axis repeated in the sky: there was
an air corridor, an air highway, the road of her dreams and
reveries, connecting West and East.

She could feel the depth of coal mines under the settlement, under the whole neighborhood, the threatening volume of giant caverns left in the ground after coal mining: it

was as if the universe itself hovered over the void here, already subsiding and ready to collapse.

And sharply, painfully, like a splinter, she felt Shaft 3/4, a vertical penetrating the worlds, connecting the underground, the earth's surface, and the sky.

Up there, in the sky, there were many people, thousands if you counted all the airplanes in a day. Down there, underground, there were many people trapped in the mine. The top ones were alive. The lower ones were dead. The upper ones didn't know about the lower ones, but they were connected by a mine shaft facing the sky. An axis. A vertical axis around which the world could turn.

Zhanna sensed that the hot air above the village was torn, drilled through with tunnels by airplanes. She sensed the presence of these migratory souls, the fickle population of the air, freely passing in airliners like birds.

And she felt, for the first time, the inexhaustible evil of the place. She recognized in it, in the locale, as one recognizes hidden rot or spoilage, that terrible, low, earthy thing that Marianna had spent her whole life washing away, not allowing it to spread, accumulate, thicken, mature, the thing that constituted a fate that would not necessarily come true, but might come true if new villains walked in the footsteps of the previous ones and shed new blood on top of the old.

She heard with horror how the earth was already wobbling, how the floors of the universe were cracking, and the middle world, the city cemetery, had already fallen into the lower world. And once again she felt that the whole area was too corroded by old mines and fresh diggings; everything here was ready to collapse, barely holding on and waiting for a push. Houses were cracking at the foundations. Meager wells were drying up. Power lines buckling. Forests dying, apple orchards shriveling. The earth was bending water pipes, taking bites out of the asphalt of roads. Cows, sheep fell into the sinkholes. And everything was covered with black sticky dust from the slag heap, with no one left to banish it.

She remembered how, when she was a child, the heap had seemed like a real mountain. It would catch fire and smoke like a volcano. They had tried to plant it with trees, but they did not take root. Then, on her one and only trip abroad, when she flew to her mother in Austria, where she worked for six months as a housekeeper and nurse to Mr. Zimmerman, the hill in the center of Graz seemed strangely familiar to her: it had the same sullen sleeping power of a dead giant as the slag heap.

Now in her dream, she found herself back at the Donetsk airport. Then, on the first flight, she was stunned and remembered it as a glassy, mirrored temple to the air, where people parted with their past, set off into the unknown of a new life; where one could so seductively and closely look at another's itinerary, printed on the ticket, and inno-cently dream of a substitution, of a fantastic opportunity to take someone else's fate, brighter, more interesting. The airport, the gateway to multiple worlds, was a glass cube like a lottery spinner—the gate numbers like the numbered balls—a cube from which stretched arrows of flights, arrows of predetermination, the space of mysticism, meetings, partings, gains, and losses.

Now the airport was empty, motionless, ruined: dead. Her dream led her past burned walls, broken, shot-out windows. In the arrival hall, small coins rolled across the floor at the ruined currency exchange counter, its lock mangled by bullets. Suddenly the conveyor belt creaked and moved, the one on the far right, the one where she had waited for her luggage a year and a half ago, in early January 2013. Suitcases began to fall through the flared rubber skirt onto the belt, with a strange thud that Zhanna could not explain. Large, heavy suitcases, luggage from a long-haul flight, all black and densely packed. Zhanna looked closely, and saw that they were no longer suitcases but coffins traveling along the belt, with a different thud, a wooden one.

Black polished coffins with gilt handles. And each had a luggage tag.

The hall faded before her eyes. Only the shiny black coffins moved, filling the space. Then they turned into a string of similarly lacquered black cars, heavy hearses driving down the twilit highway.

Where were they from? Where were they headed? Zhanna asked. And she saw something else: a huge metal hangar, and in it an airplane. A horrible, dead airplane, assembled from thousands of pieces.

The airplane was frightening precisely because of its apparent integrity, an imitation of a living machine. Destroyed, torn apart, thrown from the sky, it rose, as ghosts rise. The dead giant that brought the continents together: the jetliner that had come into being after the Cold War, the deity of a new world without borders, without confrontations, struck down by the arrow of a long-revived enmity.

Zhanna saw its death now.

Saw the impact of that fiery arrow, launched from the ground. How it exploded, piercing the fuselage. How the airplane fell on its wing, and in the fall the hull broke, the compressed capsule that held all the feelings of the world, loves, fears, deceptions, hopes; how, disintegrating, the brief forced commonwealth of destinies, memories, and languages called a flight faded away.

An impossible, unimaginable rain of dead people fell on the familiar, well-traveled surroundings of the village.

Bodies, and pieces of bodies, fell almost straight down, although they were scattered by air currents. Into fields they fell, into wheat and corn. Into deep steppe ravines overgrown with thickets. Into the vast vegetable gardens, with shriveled scarecrows in faded miner's uniforms and helmets, deterring nothing. Into cherry and apple orchards, bursting with fruit. Onto the trampled soccer field, in the heat of a game. On the buildings of the closed mine, the mine yard overgrown with grass. The black sides of the slag heap. The streets and a lot near the store, full of cars. The woods. The backyards, drying laundry, dog kennels. The overgrown fire pond where the kids went fishing. The pastures where gadfly-plagued cows and humble sheep grazed. The station where sweltering passengers waited for the bus. The mouths of diggings and dumps. The pit of the collapsed cemetery—dead to the dead.

This multiple, repetitive, agonizingly long cascade of bodies chilled Zhanna, made her suffocate in her sleep.

Dead bodies at the moment of death falling to the ground. Drowning, floating, resurfacing, given to the water. They were carried, loaded, buried, dug up. Suicides jumped and fell sometimes, but there was not much flight there. A moment or two.

Zhanna woke up: something heavy and soft had smacked the roof of the house and rolled into the front garden, making the roofing metal reverberate.

VALET

Valet's early morning started badly.

He had hoped that he would be sent to help the anti-aircraft gunners again, and there would be a chance to distinguish himself; the SAM had not appeared just randomly here, they were expecting something. Ukrainian transport planes were flying, helicopters, fighters; they were not afraid, they were not cautious, they thought the militia could have only handheld equipment. And here was the Omela, just one: not enough for an air defense system. That meant they wanted to teach them a lesson. Cut a bigger bird out of the sky.

His commander, Monk, sent him to the suburbs, to a stinking pig farm, to remind the owner that the month had long since begun, and he hadn't paid the protection money. The businessman had gone quiet and wasn't picking up the phone. "Valet, go deal with it on the spot."

He drove, trying to work himself up before the conversation. Panteleyev, the businessman, used to run the canteen at the mine. He had brought them fresh meat a couple of times when his father was crushed by a cave-in. But the hell with him, it was a different story now, old friendship didn't count. But if Panteleyev called his mother, complained, and she whispered to his father . . .

He was afraid of his father. A cripple, as immobile as a stone, who could only crap in bed and grumble, clamor, if he got angry at those fuckers who had destroyed the Soviet Union, who, therefore, were to blame for the mine collapse.

He should have died long ago, but he was alive. Valet had thought of strangling him many times before he left for Moscow. Just kill him. The whole house stank of his rot. But when he imagined putting his hands on his father's throat . . . He realized that he wouldn't be able to do it. He would only awaken his father's strength, restrained by paralysis.

And yet Valet's father had never laid a finger on him. Even though he was a blaster, a master of crushing rock, with a temper to match: dry, precise, until he went up in flames! He was the best in the whole company; the big bosses listened to him on matters of boreholes and explosives, and he was not boastful, he kept his dignity. Valet thought that if his father had ever recovered and realized what his son had become, he would have thrown him out of the house himself, and his elders, the experienced miners, would have approved.

Living in Moscow under the care of Uncle Georgy, he thought that if his father had been on his feet and in his right mind, he would have protected him from Marianna, but his mother, a cleaning woman, was accustomed to bowing to everyone. It wasn't that he wanted to go back, no, but it was nice to imagine how his father would give that bitch the brush-off . . . Now Valet understood: no way. Father would have sided with Marianna. Sometimes Valet could feel in his skin that there was a certain bond between the old miners, as if they had agreed on something long ago, underground, and they looked at him, the militiaman, the victor, the man with a gun, as if he were a mad dog.

"You're turning *Russky* fast, Valya," his fathers' friend, a former safety engineer, said coldly to him when he and the other deputies were forced out of the town council. Valet almost shot him, though what for? It was true: he was Russified; his citizenship was Russian, his service was Russian, his machine gun was Russian. But Valet didn't like reminders that he wasn't Russian by his old citizenship but Ukrainian; he had been mocked in the regiment, he had to fight, to prove with fists that he wasn't a *Khokhol*. Uncle Georgy didn't protect him in that: sort it out yourself, show yourself.

Bam, the tire slapped, the car wiggled. He had hit a nail. And no spare tire. He got out of the car. The pigsty smell came from afar. There was green corn all around, tall, fed by the recent rains; the cobs were already full, sticking out, rock hard. The town was out of sight. Just the tall slag heap, and the hot air floating above it.

Fat flies. Carried by a breeze from the farm. One landed on the windshield. Its back was emerald green. And Valet remembered how, last winter, when the demonstrators were being shoved into the truck, their fingers unhooked from the doors, a ring slipped into his palm as if by itself, a gold ring with an iridescent green stone. He then took it to a thrift shop: forty-three thousand rubles. Just right for a new cell phone, an iPhone; he was ashamed of his old one.

He had sold it then, but now he regretted it. He could have given it to Zhanna. To soften her up, make her believe him, so that his revenge would be sweeter. A ring, a brooch, a trinket, whatever else a girl needs.

Whoosh! Something chirped, snorted, rustled in the distance. Valet turned around, and a blue smoke trail vanished in the thin air above the slag heap.

At first he thought it was artillery. Ours or theirs, Ukrainian. Or a Grad rocket launcher. But the trail went steeply into the sky. Only antiaircraft missiles flew like that. He had seen one once, on a training exercise.

Omela.

He raised his head into the blinding sky and noticed a black-orange wormhole under the side of the sun: it flashed and disappeared.

A hit, Valet thought. He didn't care who. He was overcome with sudden pride, for he had pointed out the position, he had directed it!

For a few seconds nothing happened. Suddenly his eye distinguished an airplane, nose down, disintegrating in the air. A big airplane. A transport plane.

Valet jumped behind the wheel. To hell with the flat tire, as long as the car runs. There was no one around. He would be the first to get there! There could be weapons, equipment, and—hell knew what—money, important documents.

"What a rocket," he said, twisting the steering wheel, "what a rocket!"

The car drove on, the tire squelching.

He had served in the Strategic Missile Forces. He guarded multiton ballistic carcasses that were never destined to take to the air, doomed to grow old in their silos and then be dismantled. Valet remembered how the army priest, Father Grigory, had arrived one day to consecrate the launching room, walked along the top of the shaft, hummed a prayer, and splashed holy water with a white brush, and Valet swooned with bliss, for the priest was at one with the SS-18 missile, the one called Satan, and he, the soldier assigned to guard this monster, was at one with them. "Priest blessing Satan": the simple play on words delighted him, for it meant that there was really neither God nor Satan, but only the power of the rocket, which they all worshipped.

The Omela formation guarded their launching station. Their unit laughed at the anti-aircraft gunners. What they had was a cigarette, not a missile like their Satan—hello, America! The Omela really seemed so small compared to the intercontinental fool: a Skinny Minnie that didn't eat enough porridge!

But now seeing the wreckage of the huge airplane tumbling in the air, Valet was filled with involuntary respect: what they hit! He hadn't thought about the foreign soldiers who might have been in the plane. He was not going to call Monk. He had hunting fever. He almost took credit for the antiaircraft gunners' shot: If he hadn't pointed out the right place, where would they have aimed, the gawkers, where would they have fired?

The plane wreckage had already fallen. Smoke drifted over the corn. The road ran parallel to the forest, trees on the left, rows of corn on the right, and then stopped at the corner of the field and made a ninety-degree turn. Valet turned the wheel so that the car went into a skid, stepped on the gas, feeling the front-wheel drive pulling the car, and hit the brakes.

At the side of the road, in the shadow of the tall poplars, lay a pink suitcase.

Valet got out. A huge suitcase on wheels. Metal. Couldn't be any pinker.

There was something lying farther down the road. Body? Sack? Hard to tell.

The pilots must have been hustling, thought Valet. Taking passengers illegally. What was it to them, it was a big plane, a whole barn. The thought of passengers, the fools accidentally on board the plane shot down by the Omela, made him sick. Just for a second. Their own fault, he thought. It was a military plane. And fuck them, how many could there have been, two or three?

He had to race to the plane, to the huge chunks of fuselage. Search there. But opening the suitcase would only take a minute—what if it belonged to someone rich? Especially since the locks had broken in the fall. Valet reached for it and saw a luggage tag. Couldn't believe it. It was all foreign, abracadabra, AMS-KUL, and a name—how could he read it, was it in Hindu? But where was the tag from, the previous flight?

SERGEI LEBEDEV

He flung back the crushed lid. Gold glimmered inside. Facets of precious stones winked violet and ruby red at him. Wrapped in transparent paper lay a gold scepter crowned in stones, a royal cap with a ruby in the band, golden garments festooned with pearls, with wide mother-of-pearl buttons. Everything glowed, burned his eyes, shone too brightly. If they saw it they would take it away, Monk would take it, kill him, he had to hide it here, this very second. It must be from some museum or a rich guy's collection, a big shot who used to lord it over everyone in Donetsk, raking in millions from the labor of miners.

Even though Valet had been working at the digs for only two and half months, he felt like a real miner, a hard laborer who had the right to what was his. Valet grabbed the scepter, wondering what to do with it—thank God he had a car; he'd put the suitcase in the car, he had a rug in the trunk he used when he had to work under the car, he'd wrap it in the rug.

He froze. The scepter was too light. He poked it with his finger—it was plastic. It was all plastic, crap plastic, the cap, the robe . . . He dug deeper and pulled out three enormous beards one after the other: white, black, violet.

The violet one got to him. He set it aside carefully, like a grenade. What the fuck was going on? What was this shit?

Under the beards he saw a plastic folder with a design on the cover: a silver genie floating out of a lamp and beneath it a bewildering sign: International Magicians, Illusionists, and Jugglers Association. 17th Annual Congress, Kuala Lumpur, Malaysia.

Valet was furious. The *Khokhols* must have been giving a ride to some fucking magician. Lumpur, shit. Faggots, shit.

He ran to the car to drive on to where the pieces of the plane burned, where there were unambiguous trophies with no surprises.

The car wouldn't start.

In the distance, a siren blared and stuttered—either an ambulance or a fire truck. Feeling the minutes slip away, knowing Monk would be there any second, Valet ran, thinking of where to hide the loot.

On the road he found a watch, a scorched piece of sheeting, a T-shirt, swimming goggles, broken sunglasses, a keychain with keys, a blister pack of pills, a notebook, a cat carrier, a passport with a lion.

Where were the people?

He did not want to go to the broken fuselage. All the small stuff on the ground signaled very clearly: the Omela had shot down a passenger plane. A foreign plane. A transcontinental plane that flies over the town on its main route.

. . . They were always given the instructions before demonstrations: Go easy on foreigners when you arrest them; don't break their arms or legs, don't punch them in the teeth. They're white people!

There they were in the corn, the white people. And their things.

"Why the fuck did you fly here?" he said out loud. "The fuck!"

He walked over to the shattered pieces of fuselage, thinking hard about where to look for money: In bags? Inner pockets? Should he take the jewelry? Rings, earrings?

He came across bodies swollen by the impact. He avoided them for now, unwilling to rummage through everything he saw.

Absurd details caught his eye. A row of empty seats standing upright. An old woman, naked above the waist, lying on her back, legs pulled up as if waiting for her lover. Lumps, tatters, no longer possible to identify what things had been, a smoking hollow littered with charred junk, as if a garbage dump had been set on fire.

He wandered aimlessly, no horror, no compassion, collecting new unimaginable visions, the ugliness of mangled bodies and things, and feeling a strange emotionless excitement. As if he, a herder of humans used to having power over a captive crowd, had been shown a different, greater power, the power to throw from the sky to the ground, to subject the dead to humiliation, and he was measuring himself against that power, absorbing its mad compositions.

Monk and the others had arrived. He was still wandering. They wandered at first, too, commanders, bosses, not knowing what to do with that plane that had spread out over dozens of kilometers, with these foreigners who should not have been there.

It seemed that they, the corpses, were invaders, landing here like aliens from outer space. Catching the locals unawares, they had strewn themselves all around the area, occupying it.

The order came to locate and make an account of the bodies.

Valet walked at the edge of the chain of searchers combing the countryside. He didn't look at the faces closely; he photographed poses with his eyes: body parts in their indifferent separateness. He seemed to be searching for someone.

Toward evening, as the sun was setting, he drifted into an apple orchard gone wild on the outskirts of town; they used to play there when he was a kid, dragging rushes from the pond every year to build a hut. Everyone had secret spots and hiding places in the orchard. They fought and made up, smoked their first cigarettes, gulped their first vodka, retching, lit bonfires, and carved rude words and girls' names into tree trunks. Valet recalled the drunken fumbling here, the stories about incredible screwing, the older boys squeezing girls' breasts, pushing bottles of sweet homemade wine—drink, drink, it'll be better—before leading them off to the tent far away, to tumble them onto a dirty jacket.

Zhanna, thought Valet with pleasure, never went to the orchard. No one tried to get her there, to lure her: they sensed it was useless.

Valet walked, recognizing old paths, bottles in the bushes, a fresh campfire site, a tent covered in a tarp, cigarette butts, logs like benches—that meant new kids had grown up and used this place; it wasn't lost.

. . . She was lying right at the tent, facedown—as if she had been dragged here and tossed like prey. Black panties and bra: the currents that twisted and tossed her in the air had torn off her dress. Her snow-white body was covered in livid patches of bruising, but the contours were so generously feminine that Valet reached for his crotch. Spread out in the middle of the orchard, belly down, knees to the side, she was the adult submissive woman they had dreamed of while they listened to the boastful stories of Vasilek, who had served time as a juvenile for rape.

He wanted this woman from the sky—but he was afraid to touch a dead person, as if she could be dead but still ask, Where am I? Who are you, little boy? The unbroken, albeit waning, beauty of her body protected her, and Valet, hearing searchers' voices nearby, hesitated.

He looked around—should he pull her into the tent? He noticed a silvery glimmer in the tent: a small suitcase, just a carry-on, had broken the roof. It must be her makeup case: it had a citrusy scent.

In the central velvet-covered section lay a six-sided glass tube shimmering in rainbow sparkles, and inside it a golden lipstick.

Valet looked in disbelief at the price tag—1,990 euros. He took off the crystal case and pulled out the lipstick. It was as heavy as a machine gun cartridge.

Gold.

She got it at the duty-free, he thought. Brand-new.

He would give this crystal to Zhanna. Lie that he bought it for her in Moscow, saved up for months. She would believe it! Paint her lips with a dead woman's lipstick! She never used makeup, and Marianna didn't, that was their rule, he guessed, but she wouldn't be able to resist this; Marianna wouldn't be tempted, but the little one would, she would violate the rule.

He suddenly felt older, instinctively guessing what had fallen into his hands and for what. He pulled the tarp from the tent and covered the corpse, getting one last look at her nakedness—picturing Zhanna, just as immobile, submissive, waiting.

He put the lipstick crystal in his pocket, not ashamed that it was protruding.

"Found one!" He called out to the other searchers. "I found another one!"

THE GENERAL

"Fucking assholes! Idiots!" If he could have, the general would have had the gunners executed.

Did them a favor, the bitches.

Messed up the field, the fuckers.

And he had to clean up after some shitty lieutenant. Orders from Moscow: you're on the spot, general, so act.

Act, shit.

What was there to act on? The Korean Boeing wasn't enough? They wanted a second one.

There was a time when he liked to lie. He enjoyed it. It was called "propaganda support of Chekist measures." A science. He was good at it.

An engineer by education and a miner by first profession, he was able to guess the vulnerable points of structures. Points of internal stress, points of potential fracture in people. Able to read their internal pressures, their prepared defenses, their secret weaknesses. And to invent lies that not only deceived but forced a man to turn against himself, to attack his faith, to reject his principles.

Now General Korol needed a lot of lies to explain the

downed airplane. A well-crafted, first-rate story. Just like the good old days.

But it wasn't coming. It was as if the voice that spoke deceitful words had been taken away.

He knew how and what to do. He remembered, one could say, the physiology of the process, the excitement, the feeling of his own scale, arising from the scale of the idea, from the knowledge of those multiple forces that would spread this fiction, inflate it, endow it with imaginary features of reality.

He knew and he pushed and panted like an impotent man. He went over old operations as if they were images of mistresses, hoping to cling to the shadow of a former effect.

He clearly felt that he was lied out. He could no longer produce the seductive, tenacious lie. It was gone. He was bankrupt.

We were all lied out, drained, he admitted. We were naked. Whatever we came up with would not work.

But we must still deny it, the general said to himself. Deny. The main thing here is patience, and we'll endure, we'll wait it out. A major catastrophe with mass deaths, a hurricane like Katrina, or a tsunami, would help distract attention.

The war had stalled. There would be no breakthrough. The border would not move west. These republics, hastily created, were rubbish, embarrassing, homemade. Who would be interested in them? But now the whole world would be looking in this direction. It was gods who were killed here. The highest caste. Europeans.

The general never remembered dead people before, neither his own nor others. They didn't weigh him down. They never appeared in his dreams. But these, scattered across the fields, seemed to be hanging on him, making it hard to walk. And the odor, the sticky odor, he couldn't wash it off.

The smell.

So forgotten. So familiar.

The school in Beslan had smelled like that after the storming of the building and the fire. Nowhere else but in Beslan in North Ossetia, had he seen so many dead people in one place. Like these, burned, torn apart, disfigured.

Children.

Adults.

Children.

The general wrinkled his nose, remembering how all the officials had lied during the days of the seizure, lied out of order, without an overall plan, and how they had lied afterward, piling nonsense on nonsense, and it blew up in their faces: the mothers of the dead students had formed a committee to demand justice, to find out why headquarters had not negotiated, why there had been an explosion in the gymnasium, why tanks and flamethrowers had fired on the school . . . And instead of listening to his advice earlier, they gave him the task of dismantling the mothers' committee.

In general, he liked this notion very much: "measures of dismantling." The highest dramaturgy of operational work. Anyone could make an arrest. This called for undermining solidarity, breaking up an emerging grouping, debunking an idea, defaming a biography, and leaving the person to live on: dishonored and crushed. Or forcing him to speak out against his former self, to renounce like-minded people, to disavow statements. Oh, that needed imagination, a sense of plot, mastery of operational psychology.

But there, in Beslan, looking at the mothers gathered in the square, at their sorrowful unity, he first experienced a premonition of possible defeat. If his superiors had given him a year or two for the operation, he would have recruited or brought in agents, tried to split the leadership . . .

But as it was, what could you do with them? They lost their kids. They had nothing left. Nothing to hold on to. They had nothing to offer but the truth about the assault. They were almost dead themselves. You couldn't scare them. You couldn't buy them. You couldn't worm your way into their confidence.

He had the thought of pressuring the men, the fathers gripped by guilt and shame, to convince or stifle the wives. But he assumed in advance that these women would listen to no one. Not even God. And his superiors didn't want to listen: When will you deal with the women? Why are you procrastinating?

That's when he thought of Mogilny.

He had been the general's agent since the Soviet era. The general found him when the mining regions, both Donbas and Kuzbass, were paralyzed by strikes. Moscow demanded a disruption of the protest wave, a disruption of the striker coordination. The KGB had its own people in the strike committees, of course. They were gradually promoted higher and higher in the informal hierarchy, with the expectation that in a month or two they would intercept the leadership and take over the movement as a whole. But Moscow insisted: the result was needed immediately, even if it was only localized. And Lieutenant Colonel Korol traveled around the striking mines, taking a closer look, seeking out the most unstable strike committee, the weak link that would be easiest to knock out of the strike. Then the domino effect would kick in.

It was on this trip that he met Mogilny, a former lecturer of the Znanie Society promoting scientific knowledge, who had formed his own cooperative, Jupiter, and was touring mining towns giving lectures on "The True Structure of the Material and Immaterial Universe." Smack in the middle of the strike! That was the time when the country was swept up by a craze for psychics. Both old and young sat in front of the TV set, expecting their glasses of water to somehow be given magical qualities by the charlatans Chumak and Kashpirovsky during their broadcasts. The press, newly unbridled, blamed the KGB: the committee was testing technologies of suggestion and mind control. Korol was offended: You think we haven't come up with anything other than special glasses of water? This was just folk superstition, commonplace, like boogeymen and black cats.

Mogilny played at being psychic, doing magic, babbling perfect nonsense, obvious to anyone who remembered science class: energy fields, biozones, auras, anomalous locations, about Chernobyl as a proclamation of the Antichrist and AIDS as a secret weapon of world Jewry. The hall was standing room only. They knew him; he had performed there before. But Lieutenant Colonel Korol guessed his true potential. He could not recruit Mogilny right away: it was a long procedure; the candidate had to be checked out before authorization could be given. He opted for a gross violation: he introduced Mogilny into the operation without formalizing an agency relationship.

And Mogilny did not fail him. He was a born agent, a natural talent, and Korol later thought that Mogilny had not randomly gone on tour in the days of the strike: he had hoped that the KGB would notice him; he had been offering his services, showing what he could do. It took him just one evening to break up the strike committee at the Twenty-First Congress Mine, hard as flint. The strike committee members came to his talk to kick him out of town; they suspected something. He introduced the Jewish theme: let's discuss the Jewish question, whether there were more Jews down in the mine or upstairs in management. The strike committee right there in the hall, in front of a thousand people, came to blows, Brushtein shouting, "Get him off the stage," and Nesterov shouting, "Let him finish." Mogilny had nothing to do with it; he had merely brought up the topic.

He was the only one of all the agents that Korol had moved to Moscow. Mogilny did a lot of things. Then he asked to be released from the work. The general let him go. He realized he feared Mogilny. The general could destroy him, but he feared him. It was that special fear that people had of snakes, spiders, heights, or of something completely harmless: a lonely alleyway, the shadow of a tree near the house, the cry of a bird in the night.

Mogilny had an air about him. The general knew he was a charlatan, a poseur; there was nothing demonic about him. He looked like an ordinary engineer, a Soviet five-ko-peck bon vivant, a master of toasting the ladies or getting goods under the counter. Cowardly, petty, greedy for money. But sometimes, he would say two or three words to explain how exactly he was going to trample a man, and he would appear to be wise and terrible, like the serpent of Eden. What woman had nurtured him? What witches had cast spells on him? A wimp in a stinking jacket, his hair strewn with gray hair like salt, a tie with small polka dots, the face of a talent-less sweet-talker, a chatterbox, and yet. . .

The general called in Mogilny for advice.

The mothers had really gotten to him. He would watch a newsreel or a TV report: just a bunch of women, nothing simpler than that. But they had a nameless force. Something similar to what he felt in Marianna, in Snow White. An unyielding strength. Obdurate. Where could that have come from in a slavish, obedient country?

He laid it all out for Mogilny: the situation was delicate, direct pressure was excluded, they could not arrest mothers who lost their children, the public would not understand, and not just the public, the local law enforcement was unlikely to understand, the republic held a grudge against the feds, a considerable grudge.

THE LADY OF THE MINE

Mogilny tucked his nose into his palms, then massaged the nostril wings with his index fingers. He scratched the stubble on his chin. He twirled his fingers in his ears.

And he said, "You've been looking in the wrong place. There's nothing more destructive than hope. Hope is what I'm going to give them."

The general thought he'd misheard. He was counting on Mogilny to find a solution, to come up with a trick!

"What do you mean, hope?" Korol said contemptuously. "What are you talking about? What hope could they possibly have? Have you been fucking listening to me? They have nothing to live for. Their kids were killed. They want justice and we can't give it to them! What fucking hope is there?"

He thought Mogilny was crazy. He had always been a psycho, and now he was completely fucked up. He should be written off and sent to the hospital.

"Hope, hope," Mogilny repeated cheerfully, and he made a clown face.

"What hope is that?" roared Korol, growing furious.

"Hope for the revival of the children," answered Mogilny calmly, like a teacher with a dull student. "Resurrection, to be terminologically precise. I will promise them that I will be able to resurrect them. Every last one of them. Only the children. No adults. It's psychologically important."

Korol hesitated.

He didn't understand.

Then he did, and the ferocity subsided, giving way to a double feeling of superstitious fear and ecstasy, black delight, for he already knew it would work.

The idea was absurd, and there lay its greatness. Mogilny had outdone himself.

Both were silent.

And it seemed to the general that in that instant something was born into the world. A black two-headed dog. Mothers could not help but believe it. Not all of them, of course. Some of them. That was enough. The committee would be destroyed. The black two-headed dog was born.

And one day it would come for them. Both of them.

. . . They were going to give him a rank and a medal for this operation. They wanted to appoint him deputy director of the service.

Mogilny, the fool, ruined everything. He went completely off the rails, announced that he was forming the Death Abolition Party and would run for president. He hinted that he had done the president's dirty work in Beslan: the mothers appealed to him, because he was the chief. They had to put Mogilny in jail. And he was sent to the active reserve. To the television sinecure. Disgrace.

And now fate was giving the general a chance to get even, to justify himself, to serve.

He knew he was going to fail. No matter what lies he made up, no matter what hoax he started, it would all be for nothing. Not even Mogilny could help him.

But still he acted. He gave orders to run the passengers of the downed airplane through the records: God forbid some important person was aboard.

The list—stolen from the airline's database—was in front of him. The names were foreign, typed in Roman letters, but he felt they were a continuation of the Cyrillic-printed execution lists from the file he had read yesterday. And in general, the list was essentially the same: the mine connected times, connected today's dead, the shooters from the NKVD, and the murderers from the *Einsatzkommando*, as if all of them were employees of the mine, only working on different horizons, with different faces.

A car raced down the street, music blaring from the open windows, a song about criminals, something about a thief's lot. The "militiamen" were partying after searching in the fields, after a day with dead men.

The bouncy cheap melody suddenly cheered him up. All at once, he wanted to get into that car, and race, race drunk, shoot into the sky, go on a spree, forget himself.

But he ordered Semyon to drive him to the hotel. It was a pity that he had to postpone the date with Snow White.

He inhaled the night air: it smelled of smoke.

THE ENGINEER

I knew something like this would happen.

It had to happen.

Simply because of the force that came from the east. From the cold side.

I call them zombies.

They're the obsolete who don't want to become obsolete.

They were the Red Gods, victors in a world battle, worshipped on the altars of the communist faith. But when their dominion collapsed, their supernaturalism, which had hypnotized nations for nearly a century, disappeared, they, tormented by fear of the future, turned into infernal giants, monsters of the previous era, who wanted to stop time and regain their lost greatness.

Therefore, their entire war, whatever words they draped over its meaning, was about envy and revenge, the rebellion of the underdogs. Like the Jötunns of Scandinavian myths, they wanted to destroy the young gods, to take their treasures, to take the apples of youth and its inexhaustible chest.

My mine, its coal, which fed the locomotive fireboxes and open-hearth furnaces, was part of the mystery of the birth of the Red Country, the mystery of violence, the remaking of the world, the remaking of man. As I have said, coal was power. And it is not by chance that their ideological demiurges introduced the miner Stakhanov into the pantheon of heroes, Soviet demigods. He was given the gift of miraculous coal mining, which exceeded human capabilities many times over: symbolically, Stakhanov and his followers and adherents, the Stakhanovites, extracted the power of Mother Earth, the primordial element of power over the world, giving the ability to transform nature and man.

Coal, the ashes of the prehistoric era, gave birth to steel and cast iron, creating objects of power, the components of the state monster, its paws, claws, fangs: rails and cars, rifles and machine guns, artillery pieces, tanks, airplanes—everything needed to redraw borders, swallow foreign lands, exile peoples, devour human beings.

They imagined themselves to be the vanguard of humanity, renewed, better people, born, hardened, as they said, in the crucible of the bloody struggle for a new world and a bright future. But they lost, having exhausted all their reserves of violence and fear, unable to keep up with the rapid pace of time, and their once formidable state, with its coal-born military armadas, turned into a lumbering dinosaur before dying out.

The inexorable law of cosmogony has made them relics, creatures out of their era. Theirs was a war of the risen dead, a war against the flow of time and life.

"Once upon a time, at the zenith of their power, glory, and class ideology that proclaimed internationalism, they could deceive many with the idea of a universal, or even supraworldly communist brotherhood.

Today, when they were driven by the revenge of the sidelined, by the revenge of those who lost this fata morgana of universality, their bright red pelt has faded to brown.

They hadn't realized it yet, but they had turned into those whom they considered their worst enemy, whom they had defeated and crushed: the Nazis. The Nazis with their idea of exceptionalism, of a fatal chosenness, of a fateful historic battle in which a nation was doomed to fall or be reborn. They had turned into Nazis with a fetish for historical deprivation, for being robbed by others: dishonest, dodgy, and devious. With their paranoid delusions of historical grievance.

Zombies don't know they are zombies. But ignorance, blindness doesn't matter; their past atrocities, compounded by rebellion against the changed times, hang like doom over them.

That was why they shot down the plane.

That was why it was shot down at that time and in that place.

They had shot down a Boeing once before. Thirty-one years ago. When their doomed empire invaded Afghanistan, embarked on a final campaign under a red banner that was the road to the end. A passenger airliner destroyed by a missile from a fighter-interceptor was a sign of fierce powerlessness, a dying dinosaur writhing and whipping its spiky tail across the sky.

Today's Boeing was no accident.

Yes, the chain of events and commands to secretly send SAMs and give orders to shoot down Ukrainian warplanes may have seemed unintentional. But there was fate in every link of the chain. That's why the missile hit the free metal bird in the free skies, carrying peaceful travelers of all nations, the 777, the connector of continents, the symbol of the interlocked, universal, stitched together by the pathways of airliners.

The zombies bragged among themselves: "Here it is, here it is, the installation, the SAM system, capable of reaching both high and far; now we will show them, let them show their faces, let them dare, our time has come, be afraid!"

I recognized the tone of these jokes, these words, this bravado of the scoundrels. I'd heard that tone before. When they took us to Shaft 3/4.

Then they drank vodka and moonshine. They took watches and jewelry. Now they used confiscated cars to carry whiskey and cognac from looted supermarkets, loaded up TVs and furniture to send home.

Yes, they have power. But it is the power of the scum, the power of the bottom that has risen and risen. The power of a lowlife who suddenly has been given the power to rise up and rule. And that power is doomed to denounce itself. That's the law. Nature's law.

Shaft 3/4, to which we belong, is like an axis, a knife in a tree stump touched by a magic spell and over which one jumps and is transformed into a werewolf. It connects different eras and makes their similarities visible, exposing the recurring imprint of evil.

Things.

Things selected for the long journey. Their quiet traveling companionship. All the intimacy of luggage, the intimacy of a life stowed in a suitcase. The things neat or jumbled; some people packed efficiently, some in a hurry, afraid or angry, not wanting to go. Jews also went to the mine yard with things packed for a long journey into the unknown. And then the Germans and policemen would dig through this field of bags, knots, suitcases, knapsacks; there were so many of them that it was impossible to put them in one pile, and they lay in heaps.

Bodies.

Bodies that had fallen from the airplane. They would soon be removed, but there would be stains, impressions, prints, shadows. They will forever settle here, form another ghost community, a colony, in a land where there are too many ghosts already, because we, thousands of us, we once lived up there, and our houses still stand, our rooms still grow overcrowded, the trees we planted still bloom and spread their leaves.

These new dead people . . . They fell from the sky. But at the same time, it was as if the mine had vomited them out, made its hidden, terrible contents visible.

The mine.

The protean marriage of its images, each of which adds something to the essence of the phenomenon.

The mine shaft is like the barrel of an unimaginable cannon, a loaded inferno with layers of inescapable violence.

Like the vent of a volcano through which the magma of the depths rises above the summit in a plume of smoke and ash.

Like the trunk of a tree sprouting an invisible crown into the sky, a tree of three worlds. A poisoned tree, transforming everything around it for the worse.

The life-giving currents of water were broken, and therefore the streams dried up, the forests disappeared, the animals left, the fields and gardens stopped giving birth in full force. The cohesion of the earth's layers disappeared; the world began to subside, to fall, to crack, to shift—all of it—toward the catastrophe, toward nothingness.

The White Lady, the invited guardian, could only hold the slipping balance, postpone, delay the trouble, borrowing from the future.

But the war destroyed her power, for that power was the power of the *longue durée*, the power of ritual, whose purifying beneficence was based on daily, unremitting, but small effort, on repetition, on an imperceptible struggle against decay. And the war, not yet realized, still existing only as an approaching storm, crushed her first, for in order to come true, it had to pass through her: through the guardian. The zombies killed her, broke her seals, and the evil of long ago returned to the world of today. I suppose you might think I'm straying unnecessarily into the language of myth, complicating the simplicity of the bare, self-explanatory violence of war. But I am speaking from where the metaphysical roots of events can be seen.

The White Lady, the laundress of being. She washed away not only the evil of the Nazis and Soviets but the emanations of the mine as such, of all its unsettled, undissolved layers, of all the atrocities that had left deposits of uncoupled bodies. And the very evil of being uncoupled, the evil of concealment was washed away. She kept doom at bay. A genie in a bottle.

I would like to be correctly understood: it is very important for our conversation, already balancing on the verge of the impossible.

The SAMs did not shoot down the plane because the Germans and their collaborators once killed Jews here, the Soviets shot prisoners, and armies of the Civil War executed their opponents. That would be a kind of historical apology, an explanation that shifts responsibility to the forces of fate.

No. Responsibility can neither be shifted nor shared.

But it is important to realize: fate exists, and the zombies themselves awakened it, destroyed what held it back, released it into the world. Thus their doubled responsibility is even heavier. They may not have wanted to shoot down a passenger airliner, but they did everything they could to shoot it down.

And as soon as it was shot down, the recognizable pattern of the past was exposed. And the catastrophe, which had not happened a moment ago, which might not have happened if the missile had missed the airplane—the catastrophe began to happen in the force field of the terrain, in the force field of the past, and so there was a repetition, a dark echo from the well of the mine.

The invisible suddenly became visible.

Like sudden lightning.

Like a developing photograph.

In hindsight, all victims seem, as a rule, to be nonaccidental, but only because we are forced and almost unconsciously accept as an explanation the modus operandi of mass murderers, their mode of selection, their culling—accept as a given their very existence in the world, the very possibility of an encounter with them.

Thus, we reduce the victim to their stigma, to the absurd feature that guides the killers; we construct a logic of doom, and thus inadvertently recognize the killers' right to this perverse logic.

And the White Lady, the maiden of purity—and therein lies her paradox—enlightens life by holding a space in which they simply have no place, in which they do not breed; therefore, she is their main enemy.

A downed airplane, a thin tube, is like a body, beautiful, vulnerable, and therefore open to violence.

The scattered bodies and things are the imprint of chaos, a cast of the force of the explosion and the intertwining air currents.

Zombies rummage through the belongings of the dead.

Zombies take pictures on their phones.

There is rhyme and reference to the past in this, too.

When we were led to the mine, the Germans had a photographer. Frank Zimmerman. Not a war correspondent, just an amateur, a young boy, but not without talent. I know that now.

He filmed everything: how they led them, how they made them strip, how they took away the gold, how they searched them, how they brought them to the mine shaft.

How they went through the belongings they left behind.

Leica camera. Narrow Agfa film.

Exactly thirty-six frames.

Why did he do it? What strange propensity compels them to capture deeds committed by their hands?

There was one shot he thought was particularly good. He took it by climbing up the mine's headframe and leaning the camera against the metal structure. It was spring, the day was clear, and there was plenty of light. It worked, short shutter speed, sharp, clear image.

The rectangle of a frame.

The black circle of the mine shaft.

And in the center of it, shot from above, a white, naked man flying down into the darkness.

He was still alive; he was flailing his arms and legs in the air in a vain attempt to delay his fall.

But the photo's frame, even though it was documental in every grain, lies. To the viewer, the man seems to be floating, ascending upward.

Everything else, the guards, the firing squad, the crowd, is beyond the frame.

He allowed himself to print this picture, the only one on the entire roll, in his home studio after the war. He even showed it to friends and collectors as a mystery. Most people thought that the picture was taken somewhere in a wide factory chimney, and depicted the photographer's young lover, the Italian di Laggio, a talented circus gymnast.

But that was later, when he, after returning to Austria after being wounded while filming the Soviet entry into his hometown, was finally convinced that he was safe and could even afford this piquant puzzle, hiding the film in a secret compartment in his basement.

But what drove his hand in the spring of 1942, at the black vent of Shaft 3/4?

A philosopher would say photography is power. A psychiatrist would say photography is detachment.

I think they just like it.

They like to see their handiwork captured.

DAY FOUR

ZHANNA

She couldn't bring herself to go out into the yard.

Not even to look out there.

She looked out the window, but only once.

There, in her mother's untended roses, half frozen in winter because Zhanna had forgotten to cover them with straw, lay the body. The one that had rattled across the roof.

Zhanna already knew everything from local social media about the airplane. She realized that she should call an ambulance to come and take the body away.

But she couldn't do that, either.

She sat in the kitchen, running her finger over the patterns on the embroidered tablecloth, dusty and graying. She wondered if she should feel anything about the airplane. But her mother's death was still too close and it overshadowed everything else. She looked at the dishes on the stove: sometimes her mother couldn't eat at all, drinking vegetable broth; sometimes she asked for fried chicken, and then the smell made her sick, and the pots and pans seemed to remember this senseless waste of food, these rejected dishes that Zhanna had to eat for two.

In a corner of the cupboard, behind the cereals, she found a bottle of cognac that had been given to her mother about five years ago, when the laundry was still in operation. She poured it into a cup stained with tea. She drank it, intoxicated by the very smell, alien to her mother's house, violating the unwritten law.

The woman lying in the yellowed, aphid-eaten rosebushes was wearing a white blouse with a stand-up collar and blue jeans. Marianna dressed like that—the blouse and jeans were on a hanger in the closet—when she went on trivial errands, to the clinic or to the store. The woman's body was also blackened and contorted.

It was as if her mother had returned.

The misplaced, uninvited body meant: You will stay here like your mother. You will labor in vain like your mother. And you will die like your mother in long agony and oblivion.

Buried hastily, by other people, Marianna now seemed to have risen up to betray her a second time, a second time to doom her to a hopeless horror of fate.

Zhanna wanted only one thing: to disappear, to escape from this accursed guest. To erase, to wash away the stigma of her mother's heritage.

Not squeamish, having inherited her mother's tolerance, she nevertheless could not touch herself; she felt so dirty and disgusting.

She remembered something she had thought most reliably erased from memory: how her mother had woken up silently, taken the clean sheet she herself had washed from the dresser drawer, and with dark-brown feces had written a *Z* on it, crossed it out in a zigzag pattern, as she had crossed out the empty, unnecessary lines on the laundry invoices. Zhanna, already accustomed to excrement, to bad odors, then experienced the ultimate disgust, as if her mother had defiled the whiteness and herself, had crossed out the future.

The dead woman in the yard seemed to imprison Zhanna in the house.

Suddenly the oppressive presence disappeared. It was as if the voltage had gone dead in the power lines. Disbelieving, Zhanna quietly went to the door, opened the peephole.

Yes. There was only the imprint of a body in the crushed roses.

Zhanna stepped onto the porch. The red cross of an ambulance flashed in the distance. And Valet came out from behind the neighbor's house. It was like seeing him for the first time: in a swamp-colored military uniform without insignia, tall and slender, with a cheerful welcoming smile. She didn't wonder why he was wearing the uniform, why he had come home, or what he was doing here. He had spent years abroad in Moscow, and a guiding thread from him seemed to stretch away, beyond the town, away from her mother, the mine, and the dead.

Zhanna felt—desperately wanted to feel—that Valet had not returned by chance.

They used to tease him for being her sweetheart. Her mother, carefully but firmly, tried to instill fear and restraint in her. But their proximity, a common house, a yard divided by a picket fence, the friendship of their fathers, created the inevitability of mutual observation, peeping, apparently accidental scrutiny.

He, older and busy with his friends, was the nearest example of the other sex. She was wary, but she was also attracted, attracted by virtue of proximity, and guessed that it was not by chance that he was so zealous in ripping off prickly blackberries near the fence. It was not by chance that he immediately went out to dig or weed when her mother sent her to pick sea buckthorn: she climbed onto a chair, reached up, bent the unruly taut branches, and her dress was lifted, translucent, playing in the breeze.

This language of ripening fruits and berries, the language of first infatuations, suddenly returned as an image of hope. Valet gave her an apple one day. As if by chance, he held it out over the fence: "Take it, we have plenty." That year saw a good harvest of Petrov's Dessert apple.

Valet came to the porch, and Marianna's teachings came alive in her, splashing like water in a jiggling bucket. And to spite her mother, who had betrayed her, who had allowed herself this abominable death, Zhanna smiled and said, "Hello, Valya."

"I'll only be a second," Valet answered, as if a little embarrassed. "It's such a mess with this airplane. Everything's upside down."

"Thank you," Zhanna said with a look at the squashed rosebushes.

"You're welcome." Valet took another step closer, looked into her eyes diffidently. "Look, I know . . . This isn't the time. You don't have time for this. Your mother, all that stuff. But I brought you a present. From Moscow. Just take it. Maybe you'll open it later." He took a small white paper bag from his pocket and handed it to her, holding it by the string handles.

Zhanna froze: What was inside?

It wasn't that Marianna forbade her to accept gifts, or outright refused them when she was given them. But gifts, even the most insignificant trinkets, did not stay in their house. It was as if her mother drove them away; they quickly fell into disrepair, broke so that they could not be repaired, were given away, lost . . .

And certainly Marianna never allowed a gift into her inner circle, into the commonwealth of objects that served her and Zhanna every day. Knives and dishes, combs and mirrors, towels, tablecloths, clothes—everything was hand-picked, as if Marianna feared that the new object would disturb the harmony of the house, would bring foreign ways.

"Thank you." Zhanna reached out and took the gift. Only to break her mother's rule, a stupid law that never saved anyone from anything.

"I'll come back again." Valet turned and walked toward his half of the house without looking back.

Zhanna looked after him and realized that for the first time she was looking at a man with meaning, like an adult. And as an adult, she forbade herself to think why Valet had really come back, who he was now—for it might destroy her trust, her hope.

Not immediately realizing that she was copying her mother, she left the bag with the gift in the hallway, the way

Marianna used to do, letting new things rest, cool off from the road, and giving the house time to check them out.

She realized it. She brought it into the kitchen, set it on the table.

The unexpected, propriety-breaking gift captured her thoughts. Not Valet, the giver, but the gift itself. It was as if Valet were just a random deliveryman, chosen by the still unknown thing to invade her frozen, collapsed world.

She tried to sense what it was. She did not notice how the unknown object had already handed itself to her, seduced her, promising to become a sign of another future, a guide to it. As if playing, she put her fingers into the bag, felt the cold edges of the glass tube, pulled it out into the light, believing and not believing that this thing could be here in her hands, that Valet had found this treasure somewhere, guessed or divined what it might mean to Zhanna.

A glittering hexagon of crystal. A golden wand of lipstick inside. Golden shadows played in the crystal, iridescent sun sparkles or reflections of flames.

Inside, in the gilded shell, hid a color unlike any other.

Aphrodite's Scarlet.

She remembers these letters of the foreign alphabet. Golden letters embroidered on white silk, falling from a pedestal where, under spotlights, a vertical tube of lipstick without a cap shone like a jewel, shining with a sharp head, like a machine-gun bullet, in which all the shades of red converged and shimmered, but naked, shameless, inhuman scarlet reigned supreme, as if it were the tip of a sensual devil's tongue sticking out and tasting the world, emitting vibrations as subtle as the beating of bumblebee wings, wanting to penetrate deeper.

Around the golden wand, a crowd of customers moved in a slow circle dance, attracted by the ruby-scarlet drop. Rotating glass floors, running staircases, shimmering showcases full of riches. Own it, put on some lipstick, say the word, and things will obey, come at your beck and call, flow in flocks: fur coats and watches, handbags and necklaces. Yes, take it! Color your lips, say a word, and your speech will sound different, and your words will have a different power; all will listen to you and submit to your will. Take it and the very city of Graz, celebrating Christmas, ringing its bells, juggling houses and alleys, will obey you, all its frantic merry-go-rounds, its straw-lined crèches, all its air redolent of mulled wine and cheeses, streetcars running into the night with yellow, beady-eyed lanterns so similar to miner's lamps.

Aphrodite's Scarlet, gold wand, gold emblem, gold series. The most expensive lipstick in the world. The matchless color of the world! Stinging and stabbing, the color of passion and suffering! All is flesh, all is blood, agony, torment, atrocity, duplicity, and inevitability!

Oh, how it had scorched her two years ago, sixteen years old, unkissed, avoiding other people's fun, other people's loud language, the strange city, where her mother had only a temporary room on the top floor of an old mansion, whose owner she was nursing.

Zhanna had flown in for a vacation. She was secretly wary of this place, not understanding why Marianna, who, after the mine and laundry closed, had refused offers of part-time work in Europe, suddenly changed her mind and agreed to become an attendant. A woman, one of her mother's rare sister-friends, had come one evening, gaunt and wrung out, and they whispered in the kitchen, and Marianna started packing her suitcase.

. . . Her mother let her go out alone. Lost in the merry city, Zhanna wandered in solitude, made anxious by the mansion with its turrets and twisting staircases, frozen in a strange, unnatural cleanliness, as if dust were not born in it, as if things did not wear out; by the lifeless air of the rooms, as if in a mine drift without ventilation; by the mute and motionless body beneath the satin blanket she saw through the slightly opened door, the body of Mr. Zimmerman, the master of the mansion, paralyzed for years, the childless scion of a wealthy family, the owner of vineyards that had ceased to produce and of a ski resort from which the snow had gone forever . . . How did her mother know all this? Why was she telling her? Who, in fact, allowed her to bring Zhanna here, to the sad house of a dying man, and why did Marianna behave as if she were in charge? How did she understand the locals if she had learned only three dozen words in German, and how was it that the servants recognized her will, her right, without being aware that they were obeying her? In confused loneliness Zhanna went into a department store, drawn into the slow human whirlpool around the lipstick, stung, mesmerized by the glow of scarlet and gold. She experienced a sudden temptation, unfelt by others, addressed to her personally, to touch her lips with lipstick, to redraw her face and her fate, to become her own person here, to twist the city around her.

She felt that if she could just go and take the lipstick, no one would stop her; in the Christmas revelry everyone would consider it a performance, Cinderella coming for cosmetics for the ball. Zhanna took a step, another, but from inside, from a long-standing, ancestral, female depth, came the prohibition as goosebumps, a bodily echo: do not.

Neither her mother nor her grandmother ever wore cosmetics. But they never looked bad. On the contrary, it seemed that there was some makeup on them, a glow of knowledge and prosperity, something from the light of spring raindrops, from the tenderness of the first sprouts, from the gloss of ripening apples. Mother never even had a makeup bag. She told Zhanna, "Wait, your hour will come, your time of beauty," but Zhanna was in a hurry; she saw how pale and unattractive she was. She knew the adult, early steadiness of her hand in drawing, and wanted to try it on herself. She tried on her classmates' makeup, but it was useless: horror, not a face.

She looked at the lipstick, imagined using it on her lips, looking at herself in the mirror, and seeing a scarlet, adult smile, the princess who belonged to this city. But she realized that she wouldn't dare, wouldn't approach, wouldn't take it. And the opportunity was slipping away, and in a few minutes, it would be gone.

She walked obediently out of the store, swallowing her resentment. She crossed the bridge over the river, looked back. She suddenly saw that Schlossberg, the fortress hill guarding Graz, looked remarkably and inevitably like a slag heap. Just like the one that towered over her town.

It was as if Zhanna's vision had been switched, and Graz, too, appeared as a town-by-a-hill, an appendage to it.

Here there was the clock on the tower under the black angular roof. There, the clock was on the tower of the ore mining plant, which used to measure the time of shifts, time under and above ground.

Schlossberg was permeated with tunnels, as the ground beneath the village was permeated with drifts. The elevator whose shaft was cut into the rock and lifted tourists and revelers to the top was like the mine cage lifting miners from the depths. She was intuitively familiar with this play of space, of top and bottom, and the tunnels breathed familiarly with the dampness of stone.

Schlossberg, pierced also by the verticality of the fortress well, lowered to the level of the river, the well from which the besieged drew water during the siege. Yes, yes, the way the city was pierced, riddled, its arches, its narrow streets like drifts, its street-food carts like mine cars, its streetcars shining with the soft yellow light of miner's lamps.

Schlossberg. Its tunnels had been cut in the war to serve as bomb shelters—Zhanna had read that in a guidebook. They were laid out to accommodate the volume of people expected. Engineers, surveyors like her father, had calculated that. The hill was meant to hide, to absorb the whole city, everyone living in it.

And now it resonated in Zhanna with an agonizing shiver of recognition at the thought of tunnels stuffed with people.

When Zhanna returned to the house, she thought she had managed to hide her disappointment and resentment over the lipstick. But Marianna sensed it. She made her tell everything. And without scolding, without even lifting an eyebrow, she said, "Tomorrow we'll do a thorough cleaning together."

It was a strange process. The house stood devoid of dust for some reason, as if frozen in time, stopped by the owner's paralysis. But her mother cleaned, scrubbed, washed as if the rooms, corridors, furniture, and carpets were full of grime and stains; she used a rag like a planer stripping the bark off a log. Zhanna, repeating her movements, got carried away, and sometimes it seemed to her that something was really being washed away, peeled, scrubbed, something invisible, some old deposits, shadows, imprints of long-ago footsteps, incorporeal ashes of thoughts, patina of existence. She and her mother were doing something so that the house would be clean for the next owners, who would succeed the dying Zimmerman, who had no heirs. Free of the past.

The house was huge, excessive. Zhanna imagined she felt the different characters of the rooms vacated when family members passed away: something ineffable, accessible only to wet fingertips. The house was full of menacing emptiness and twilight, sunken minutes, rays of the day before yesterday's sunset, lost in the depths of the mirrors. At the beginning of the work, Zhanna had thought it would take three days, but they finished by evening, as if this day held more time than the others.

It was only after exhaling, looking around, feeling tired that Zhanna realized that her mother had outsmarted her: the scarlet tongue of lipstick, the outlandish flower, had faded, almost disembodied in her memory, as if Zhanna, scraping the floors, scrubbing the furniture, had unwittingly torn it away from herself.

The rooms were still breathing with the excitement of cleaning, and she walked through them as if to check for loose ends. She had seen something, something important, as she scrubbed and rubbed.

A painting?

A sculpture?

Three walls of the study were covered with bookcases. Books long unread, tightly squeezed into the shelves, seemed to have stuck together, glued, becoming solid bookends. The fourth wall was vacant, and on it hung a photograph: a white, naked man, arms and legs spread, floating above a circle of blackness. It seemed to her that she knew the image from somewhere. It had something to do with her, with her and her mother.

White on black. A naked male body, an old photo. An old house, an old town, a paralyzed old man in bed. Was he flying in the shot, free, nimble, like an acrobat?

She walked out to the spiral staircase. She looked down,

and suddenly the well of the staircase turned into an abyss, sending a sharp fear of falling, the cold spirit of the abyss, and disappearing.

As she fell asleep, she saw the scarlet beacon of lipstick disappear in the darkness, like a beacon on the wing of an airplane flying off into the night. She returned home after the vacation and forgot about the lipstick. And soon her mother returned: old Zimmerman had died, as if they had inadvertently swept away the rest of his life with their cleaning.

And now Aphrodite's Scarlet, that lipstick, as if it had fallen to her from heaven, was returned by the hands of Valet, the fool who had not even realized what he had purchased. But how could he have bought it? Zhanna remembered how much it cost. A fake?

Of course, it must be fake.

She felt empty and light. And even a little funny: she had believed it, silly girl. Born and raised in the world of cheapness, in the world of Chinese copies, in the world of "Adibas," she was put in her place.

Aphrodite's Scarlet, sure! It was as if her mother were still watching over her, wouldn't let her be tempted.

And already knowing for sure that the color would not be the right one, the only one, the one worth a thousand, she thoughtlessly opened the crystal hexagon, took out the wand, removed the cap, and twisted, rolled up the tip of the lipstick, pointed like the tip of a rocket.

It seemed to her that with that movement the world turned around the axis of the wand: the slag heap and the cemetery, the mine and the village, the clouds in the sky and the mine drifts deep in the earth.

This was it. The real one.

Aphrodite's Scarlet.

Scarlet so fresh, so bright that the lipstick tongue seemed alive.

Alive, touch your lips to it, kiss it gently, and it will respond, color your lips with an impossible, irresistible, brilliant, fatal shade: banal words from commercials suddenly acquired a direct, absolute meaning.

Looking at the lipstick, feeling the golden wand in her fingers, so attractively close to her lips, already open, already ready, she ran the sensitive pad of her index finger over them to feel their sensitivity, their anticipation. To recognize them as the new Zhanna, the one who would be gone, away from here forever.

The lipstick loomed before her eyes like a bullet: only one and it could decide everything. How little there was of it! How quickly it would run out! But now it couldn't be closed, put away, saved. It would fade, lose its magic. Here and now, make up your mind. And then the scarlet lips would tell her who: Valet? Someone else? Words that would open new paths.

She held the wand up to her eyes, to enjoy its untouched color once more. But up close, it was as if the color opened its gut, revealed what it was made of: a wild mixture of vile flesh and refuse, crocodile entrails, bat droppings, frog eyes, foam from bulls' nostrils, mad dog semen, scorpion stings, spiderwebs, fly legs, swamp fly agaric, and its bright scarlet was an obsession of madness, an evil mirage that blinds the eyes.

In that instant she guessed where the lipstick had come from. The only way it could have gotten into Valet's hands. Maybe from the duty-free on board? she said to herself. So it belonged to no one? And she answered herself: it was unlikely that Aphrodite's Scarlet would be sold on airplanes. It's someone else's. From someone else's luggage.

Unused, but it belonged to someone.

So it was stolen.

Marianna would have taken it away. Burned it in the oven.

But there was no Marianna.

Could this be the only way to rewrite life? she asked herself. Only by taking someone else's? Was that the secret? That you had to commit a sin? To desire what you can't have? She had to hurry: it was as if a field of dangerous miracles had spread around her, and only now could someone like Valet give an illicit gift to someone like her.

Zhanna put the lipstick on the table. Vertically, like a candle. She remembered an evening last summer, the night before she left for her studies. An August evening when the falling stars and flying airplanes had awakened an uncomfortable longing: as if there were short-lived moments when one could suddenly become someone else, steal someone else's life, someone else's fate. And the part of her soul that knew and could do it, the secret, tenacious, clever, evil part, woke up at that moment. It jostled like a child in the womb, testing its mistress's feelings, its reaction to her presence. Zhanna's love of burning meteors, of wastelands, of untended places—as if she had indeed picked up a piece of another's wandering soul, a homeless wanderer of the twilight—suddenly appeared in this frank, thieving sensation.

And accepting its truth, its power, Zhanna took the lipstick and outlined her lips, from left to right and back again, opened her mouth wider, gently touched the pillows in the center with the acutely angled lipstick tongue, then the corners of her mouth.

She went to the mirror in the living room, her mother's mirror, uncovered. She saw herself as if in shadow, in soft focus. Only her lips were clear, bright, delineated, unadulterated scarlet, a scarlet smile that was separate from her blurred face: lips ready to kiss, connecting her, flesh to flesh, with the future.

And she kissed herself in the mirror, as if passing through it, leaving her old self in the room, reincarnating. She undressed: for the first time, as if for someone, evaluating, lusting. An adult. Not a boy like Valet. In the mirror, her body, thin, white, unloved, suddenly acquired an anxious grace, eager to touch, to embrace, and she herself wanted to dance with this maiden in the mirror, to throw her into giddiness, into a self-indulgent intoxication.

A few simple, timid steps, and she stopped, realizing that her body, dormant since winter, had accumulated pent-up, unspent energy, and she was looking for rhythm, space, platform, music. The smile on her painted lips was already dancing.

Feeling her nakedness like a kiss of electrified air, she pulled out of the closet a dress made by Aunt Luda, a dressmaker friend of her mother's, that she had worn at the prom.

Her mother had washed and put it away afterward.

The dress was neat, white, just below the knee: for the chaste dances watched by teachers and parents in the assembly hall. But now, two years after the measurements had been taken, it fit differently, teasingly hinting at a bride's attire. White, simple, it made the figure attractive but anonymous, forcing the eyes to rise higher, to the hollow of the lips, a mysterious shell form, invitingly glowing scarlet.

Zhanna thought angrily, resolutely, as if still defending herself in an absentee argument with her mother, that she was not to blame. The downed airplane, the dead passengers—she had nothing to do with them. The lipstick came to her by accident. The accident pardoned her. Out of the misfortune of others, good was born for Zhanna, and she had to take it, for this was how life offered her the path of salvation.

Her mother and grandmother found and married their own selfless husbands. She would do the same. Somewhere in the town full of men who were strangers to this place, there was someone who would choose her and take her away. The war had trapped her here, and the war would set her free. Since her mother had betrayed her, she would have war as stepmother. For a little while, for a day, for two days, just to get out, not step onto the trail of her mother's fate.

At that instant a long trill rang, the doorbell she had been subconsciously awaiting. Valet stood on the porch.

She had not expected him. It seemed to her that his part was over. He would find out only later that Zhanna had gone off with someone else. Well, he wanted to take her out. He couldn't stand it; he had come to see how his gift was working.

Oh, it was working. You couldn't even imagine how well.

But you would see soon enough.

You came all serious, a man in camouflage, a thief, a looter. You've come to claim what's yours.

Take me where you want to go, neighbor boy, Valetik, you fool.

Drive without realizing you're not taking me for yourself.

She opened the door.

VALET

When Valet arrived from Moscow, the town was the same as the day he had left six years ago: gloomy and wary. They, pretending to be conscientious citizens, fighters who had formed into a militia on their own, stood with the anti-Maidan pro-Russian agitators, seized the police station, the city council, and shouted into a megaphone that "the people are with us." But the people shunned them, regarded them apprehensively, and if the people had realized in time, had been able to organize themselves, there was no telling who would be in power today.

He could feel this discontent fermenting. It was fermenting but incompletely. He recognized his father's friends on the streets. And they pretended not to recognize him. If he said, "I'm Valentin, the son of Leonid, Lenka the blaster," they'd say, "Sorry, kid, I don't remember." He wanted them to recognize him, respect him, even fawn over him, but they gave him the silent treatment.

At rallies, they were told about the republic, about the centuries-old friendship with Russia, about the fight against Nazism, and they said, "Is Moscow going to appoint our bosses again?"

To be honest, in the first month Valet did not believe that things would work out. He had expected to see fear, submission, and adoration from the very first days: Moscow has come. Although it could not be said officially, people understood where the weapons came from, where the orders came from. But they were looked at without respect, only with apprehension, like they were raving idiots, drug addicts, tripping on bath salts. If you looked at the town, walked the streets, went into the yards, listened to what people said, you would never believe they were seriously thinking of separating from Ukraine.

Valet was already used to being obeyed unconditionally, if not respected. He was used to the crowd obeying him, not showing its temper, allowing its hands to be twisted, not looking him in the eyes. The crowd was afraid. Maybe not showing it, but afraid. Waving placards, chanting speeches, saying, we are the power here. But when it came to violence, it immediately retreated, breaking ranks, letting the cosmonauts take a person without complaint, filming everything on phones and posting the photos, making the work of the operatives easier. But here. It was different here. Not like in Russia.

Valet even wished then that someone would stick his neck out, come out with a Berdan rifle; then he could show his strength openly, shredding the man with a line of bullets. He was a little embarrassed that he had never been in combat, had never fired an automatic at people: only in the army at target practice.

It finally dawned on Valet how it worked. No one had believed in the republics; they thought it was all nonsense, a clown show that would die out on its own. And now it was too late to complain, because life had changed unnoticed. It had new rules. New money. Even the language was different: the bazaar spoke a different language now, new words brought by the "volunteers," which traders adopted. Different bars opened, like the Paradise, and dealers recognized the need and catered to the demand.

At night, vehicles that didn't exist traveled the roads. Trains came to the station, bringing shells that weren't there. For the guns and multiple rocket launchers that were also not there. And no problem, the trains were received and unloaded, soldiers were served in stores and cafes. No more sidelong glances.

It would be different with Zhanna, he thought. Zhanna would fall in love. She had to. Such a gift! He had to go to her today. The girl would be impatient, she would open it, be stunned; her mother never spoiled her, and here she had this. He would go, later, in the evening, and take her to the Paradise; he had money, he had found some in the pockets of passengers, had taken it straight to the exchange point.

He decided to wash not in the shower, which was filled with rust, the repairs going on for months, but in the banya, without heating it. He drew water from the well, rejoicing in the strength of his hands, doused himself, soaped, rinsed with icy water, and sat down on the bench, recalling the banya in Uncle Georgy's country house, a general's bathhouse, even though his uncle was a lieutenant-colonel. The logs were brought from Siberia, cedar, for the right fragrance, and the logs were very thick; the stove, the heater, was covered with granite cobblestones, heavy, rough, dark red, like slices of meat. His uncle sometimes invited select coworkers to that bathhouse, not chosen for their rank but for their loyalty. He had his own guard, his own special team in the regiment, old men with whom he had fought in Chechnya. There, in the banya, they made their decisions. And Valet, the junior, ran errands, brought beer, added steam, replaced a worn-out leafy whisk. It wasn't much of a job, more like a waiter. But Valet appreciated the trust, he realized that his uncle was singling him out, bringing him into his circle; a lot of things were discussed there that the rank and file shouldn't know, orders from above, instructions for journalists and diplomats. But most importantly, the officers remembered the war, and Valet listened, committed things to memory, because he wanted to be like them. Perhaps his presence loosened their tongues; everyone wanted to teach the lieutenant-colonel's nephew about life in a benign way.

They washed frantically, lashed with vigor, as if they were washing something off but could not, they wanted to remove something from their skin, from their hands, from under their fingernails; they steamed until they fainted, pushing on the shelves so that sweat poured down and their guts were refreshed. In the hot steam, he saw flashes of flushed, swollen faces, hairy arms and legs. In the hot steam, visions of the past were born out of scant words.

One in particular came to mind now.

Uncle Georgy had told the story. They were walking through the forest in the mountains, returning from a raid, and in the ruins of an old village, evacuated back under the tsar, destroyed, only hulks of stone masonry remaining, they came upon some shepherds. The clouds had slid down the slope, dissipating, muffling sound, hanging shrouds between the trees, so they saw them only when they were on top of them; one shepherd jumped up quickly, as if he was going to shoot, and they used their automatic rifles and killed all five shepherds.

And then they recognized who they were. Two weeks earlier, the soldiers had stolen a lamb from these shepherds who had come to the well. The village was uninhabited, but the well had survived. It was deep, inlaid with stone, too dark to see the water but if you tossed in a pebble it fell for a long time before its splash echoed back. The shepherds had a leather bucket and a rope to get water. But they didn't have time to drink it.

Uncle Georgy said he was angry at this well, at the whole abandoned settlement. Our soldiers had crushed the village a hundred fifty years ago, but look closely and you could see where the houses stood, where the mosque had been, the square was, where the meadows were edged by the river, even though everything was overgrown with forest. And the well was alive, though it should have collapsed, warped, and withered.

The uncle ordered the corpses to be dragged and thrown into the well, so that it would be poisoned forever, and no one would ever take a sip of its water again. Not everyone in the group, the uncle said, understood the order. They obeyed. They didn't say a word. But it was obvious that they felt sorry about the well. They didn't pity the shepherds, but they pitied the well. "And then," said his uncle, "I realized that in this war you can rely only on men who are ready to kill the well, to kill the land itself, so that nothing else will grow on it, and no memory will remain."

The bodies of shepherds, then, fell into the well like the bodies of Jews into the mine, he thought without elaborating on it. He left the thought as one would leave a burning cigarette lit as a momentary distraction. He told himself, for the tenth time, that Uncle Georgy was not mistaken in him, and he would not spare the well, if necessary. He imagined how he would have the same house as Uncle Georgy's, the same luxurious, cleverly built banya, and he would gather his fellow officers there, a lieutenant-colonel like his uncle, and maybe even a major-general. He would tell them how he hid the Omela in the ruins of the mine, how they searched for passengers in the fields and forests.

But he realized he would never tell anyone about Zhanna.

He would take her to the Paradise. He would get her drunk on their cocktails. The locals would recognize Zhanna; they would understand who brought her and why, right after her mother's death. He had to choose the time so that the Paradise was full—although there was always a crowd there—so that everyone had time to drool, to appreciate the babe. Then he would fuck her at home, where Marianna had lain dying. And in the morning . . .

Would Zhanna have a morning? Valet thought. He had just seen dozens of murdered women, mutilated and whole, chaste and shamelessly naked. His mind had taken from each body fragments of poses, facial expressions, assembling the image of the dead Zhanna. He realized that this was the kind of revenge he wanted, and he could do it: there were too many deaths around, too great a fuss with the plane, and Zhanna lived alone, and no one would ask where she was, maybe she had buried her mother and left, maybe . . . Even if she was captured by the cameras at the Paradise, it didn't matter; no one would look for her, they'd say she disappeared, nothing to do with him, he had walked her home, that's all.

Greetings, old Marianna.

Warm greetings.

When he rang the bell, he was sure that Zhanna would be wearing house clothes and he would have to coax her, tell her she needed to relax and rest.

Yet she flung open the door all dressed up. Valet grew wary, sensing something strange. Herself? Without coaxing?

She had used the dead woman's lipstick. That scarlet smile, glowing and illegal, hid the face behind it. It was not Zhanna before him, and the imprint, the drawing of red lips hanging in the air, belonged and did not belong to her, making her alien, unattainable, older.

He pictured them at the Paradise, Zhanna in a white dress and her innocent lips outlined in whorish red lipstick.

Then he would bring her home; she was just a simple girl who did not know life, she had dressed up to look older, he would bring her home and . . . The body at the end of the tunnel flashed before his eyes, made up of images from these past few days, dead arms, legs, hips, and breasts.

He said in a calm and friendly way, "Why don't we go out for a bit? Sit somewhere. Toast her memory. In a neighborly way." Valet didn't know what else to say. The scarlet smile was confusing him. He had assumed Zhanna would use the lipstick. But he thought it would look inviting, like that of a novice slut.

This red smile meant something completely different.

"Let's do that," Zhanna replied. "Thank you for coming." She came down from the porch, moved a step closer to him, and he smelled the lipstick: sweet and intoxicating, like wine.

They knew Valet at the Paradise, of course. The staff was good at determining and remembering where people came from, who they belonged to, calculating their significance and authority, whether they made trouble and reached for guns. They knew him, but that was all Valet could count on; his rating was beginner level, like in a computer game in an arcade. He was a bit worried that there would be no table—every boss kept his own, where strangers could not be seated, and the remaining tables were allocated by the waiters according to rank. He was in luck: the bartender was Grinya, a school pal who used to play with him in the abandoned apple orchard. Grinya didn't recognize Zhanna

in her scarlet makeup. He raised his eyebrows and gave
Valet a discreet thumbs-up for landing a babe like that, and
then whispered a word to the waiter. There was one table
for two, by the window between the palm trees, and they
were seated there.

Valet thought that Zhanna would start talking, say thank
you, and the rest would just flow. But she sat there, bewildered, as if not quite sure why she was there, why her determination had brought her to this place. She ordered the first
thing on the menu, a plain Margherita pizza, and Valet barely
got her to have a drink, and that was crap, too, a piña colada:
he could only hope that Grinya would pour the rum with a
heavy hand.

The restaurant was gradually filling up. Out of the corner
of his eye, Valet kept track of the cars pulling into the parking
lot. He recognized them. Many had different owners when
winter started. For example, Monk's Land Cruiser—it had
been taken away from the coal reseller; Valet saw how the
owner did not make a fuss and just handed over the keys. The
Nissan Patrol driven by Boba, commander of the Cossack
battalion, was taken with blood. The market owner did not
want to part with it and had threatened them with the criminals who protected him.

The stars were out of alignment. Valet had planned to
have a quiet evening and get Zhanna drunk, but important
people were coming in. They were bitter enemies; Monk
couldn't stand Boba and vice versa. Militiamen. Army men.
Bandits who joined forces with the FSB, and each had his own

crowd, bodyguards, flunkies. Zhanna was sawing away at her pizza, pretentiously eating pieces with a fork, unhurriedly, barely touching her cocktail, and looking at him politely, in a snobbish way: Why aren't you amusing me, since you invited me? Marianna could have given him that look, the aristocratic bitch.

Valet, who was a fighter—after all Uncle Georgy had taught him a thing or two—was picking up bad vibes. He squinted at the room: they were looking Zhanna over. Not staring; there wasn't anything to stare at, she didn't have that kind of figure, but they were looking. Boba threw her a glance. Mamont, a man from the Caucasus, looked at her over his shoulder. So were other men, some acquaintances, some strangers. Like a breeze moving through the crowd.

They were looking at her lips.

There were girls at the nightclub. How could there not be. Select. Straight from the beauty salon—it was nearby, called Charm—their faces all painted; they say the beauticians were brought from Moscow. Their dresses were from Donetsk, from the local boutiques, necklaces and earrings from there, too. But you couldn't see their splendor. They sat there, sulky, gray, as if sprinkled with ashes or coal dust. But Zhanna's lips glowed blindingly scarlet. They seemed to whisper something to every man in the place.

Something different to each one.

Valet, who had never witnessed this among humans, only dogs, guessed that the hounds were stretching muscles, stirring, growling in anticipation of a canine wedding. It was

Zhanna, the bitch, the bitch that had enchanted them—he didn't know how, she wasn't worth the senior men fighting over her. It was too late to leave, to pretend that they had eaten and were going home.

But the men in the bar wouldn't let them go.

Wait, calm down. She was with him. He was one of Monk's men. Monk knew who his uncle was. Uncle Georgy would make them pay for his nephew, for his own blood, if something happened.

A waiter came over with a bottle of champagne in a bucket, another one brought a rose bouquet, tables and chairs were moved screechingly over the wooden floor, and Boba headed straight for their table, and said, never looking at Valet, "Come over to our table, sweetie. It's more fun with us."

Zhanna, the slut, got up and went, bringing along her red smile. Boba finally paid attention to Valet with a smirk: What're you going to do about it, boyfriend?

Valet tried to catch Monk's eye, hoping that he would step in. Valet was unable to stand up or say a word. But Monk did not see him. He was looking at Zhanna, too.

Valet realized that if he made a fuss now, there would be big trouble. An hour ago, he thought half the place were his people. Now they were all strangers, even Grinya at the bar. They would take him outside, for a talk. There was a small park around the corner; fools who had wandered into the militia's hangout by accident were often thrown there. In the morning there would be nothing but blood and shreds of clothing. If he sat there, frozen like a rabbit, no one would touch him. They weren't interested in him now.

All eyes were on Zhanna.

What a bitch!

Following someone's order, the guards moved the tables. The red and violet strobe lights went on; the mirrored ball on the ceiling started turning, faster and faster, showering patches of light, looking like silver pockmarks on faces, like bullet holes in walls. Music poured in, blasting through the speakers: *You're my heart, you're my soul.* Monk led Zhanna away from Boba's table onto the dance floor, and Boba did not interfere.

Monk expected her to dance with him. But Zhanna moved the men's circle away from her, widened it with her arms, and they stepped back, giving her room. She danced by herself and with them all, the bride of all, the bride of war. Her body in the white dress dissolved in movement, and the smile—like a burning red coal—danced separately. The crowd was howling, come on, come on, burn! He felt that time stood still, and Zhanna had been dancing a minute—or an hour: a stream of river water that could not be impeded flowed through the girlish figure, the breath of ebbing and receding foam.

Impotent, and wanting someone—Boba or Monk, or anyone at all—to violate her, to wipe that spellbinding red smile from her lips, to bruise them, smash them, to teach her her place, Valet suddenly realized: it was Marianna dancing. The mother, in the daughter.

The commanders stretched out their pleasure. Let her dance herself out; more pleasurable that way.

Time stood still.

Zhanna danced.

THE GENERAL

There had been a problem with the Koreans, too, but it turned out better, thought the general. Much better. They shot it down over the sea and everything was lost in the water. Deny whatever you want, send ships here and there, simulate a search. But here . . . the steppe was as open as a table.

He was back in his old office. The Omela, that damned thing, was taken back to where it came from. Moscow now wanted to know how many people had seen it. Half the region had. The Omela was not hidden; it drove around showing off: take a look at what we have.

The general was supposed to be working, planning a cover-up, but he was thinking about the Boeings. The first was a 747, this one a 777. KAL 007, MN 17. Sevens everywhere.

Of course, half the world flew on Boeings. It was no surprise they hit one a second time. But they had hit it! The specialist explained to the general that they had taken the liner for a military target. The army men were strangely calm, as if the fact of inadvertence excused them. They did not understand the consequences.

He had a strange feeling: it wasn't numbness but a detachment from what was happening, a total indifference to the current orders. And there was an exhausting, morbid interest in why his personal fate had brought him back here.

Thirty years ago he was here, in the settlement of Marat. In this office, with a view of the slag heap, this antiquated safe in which the NKVD operatives of old had kept their interrogation reports. It was August, the hottest of Augusts, he had returned from vacation and treated his coworkers to beer in the cafeteria, which was now—what was it called? The Paradise. Good, bitter beer. It was brewed locally: everything for the miners, for the hegemonic class. And then TASS reported on September 3rd: a plane violated the border and vanished; we don't know where. Their department had its orders: increase vigilance, cut off rumors, take the most active babblers under operational surveillance.

And now many years later, he was back in the same office with the same safe. With the same old archives left here. And the new operational records from the Security Service of Ukraine. With new agents that had to be destroyed or rerecruited. You could say that he was back in the past, where he had once wanted to go so badly, where there was no independent Ukraine, and even though he was of low rank he felt he was part of a power much greater and more majestic than the Russian one, with its double-headed eagle and tricolor flag, under which he now served as major-general.

Yes, he was back in the past. Or the past had come back. But why did he think that this time would be better? That there wouldn't be any idiotic mistakes, none of the general lackadaisicalness that made the Union disintegrate. It seemed they had learned a few things. Afghanistan taught them, Chechnya taught them. Ossetia and Abkhazia. The Trans-Dniester.

Think how well they took Crimea: clean, precise. On a platter.

And now this: another Boeing.

Maybe it looked different in Moscow. But sitting in the office where he had once planned the first recruitments, the general understood what the Boeing meant. It was a sign: nothing would ever be different. He wanted the past—the past was here. Just the way it had been. Not the refurbished, sweetened past they fed television viewers with all those series about the golden Soviet years. But the real, fatal, mediocre past. He thought of one of the last investigative cases here. They were planning an open pit and designed an enormous excavator, which they brought over in parts, assembled it, and discovered it could not move. It sank. Destroyed every kind of ground. The general had seen its carcass on the way to the settlement; even the ubiquitous metal hunters couldn't handle it.

Back then, in 1983, he heard the blatant lies the Ministry of Internal Affairs told on the radio about the Korean Boeing and thought what a bunch of idiots, dolts, and useless old farts they were! If they had trusted him to do it, it would have been a hundred times better. His lie would fit like a British bespoke suit; you could wear it without losing face. These guys could use only the patterns from the Bolshevichka factory, and they didn't even sew it; they hammered it out of plywood!

Well, now he was "them." Over the decades they seemed to have learned to lie in a modern way, wisely, stylishly. With flare, spark, and imagination, without that Soviet grayness. They spent a quarter of a century pulling the wool over people's eyes: democracy, a new Russia . . .

But why was it that now, when a clever lie was needed more than ever, he didn't feel like lying? Colonel Onoprienko, who worked all his life in the Fifth Department, covering the Moscow circuses, making sure that they didn't let any anti-Soviet material creep into their performance, told him about an experienced magician, a master of his craft, who stumbled over something simple and lost his nerve; his whole act fell apart—the doves didn't fly out and cards didn't jump from sleeve to sleeve. Why does he feel like that lousy magician? Just because this was a second Boeing and no one would believe the ones who shot down the first?

Too bad we never did open Shaft 3/4, he thought. We could play that card. Blame the Ukrainians. Something along the lines of: "In the same place where German fascists committed a monstrously evil act in 1942, a new crime was committed by contemporary fascists."

He listened closely. Committed—committed. Repetition.

In fact, the whole phrase sounded . . . It sounded ambivalent.

The general laughed: he had exposed himself.

But the phrase stuck. Whirled in his head. He remembered a conference in Kyiv where they discussed how to compromise Ukrainian nationalists. A senior colleague, from espionage, shared his experience of a long-ago operation where they painted swastikas on synagogues in West Germany. To show the revival of fascism. He said they bought black paint, the most common brand, housepainter's brushes, also the cheapest sort, arrived by night, no cameras back then—and go, six strokes and you're done. Couldn't have cost more than one hundred Deutschmarks, but the effect... Then-Colonel Korol listened and thought, I wonder how they felt; they were Soviet men, after all. A swastika. And if they had been caught, it would have been a world scandal, Soviet officers, with diplomatic status, on the eve of Kristallnacht.

Why didn't they have local agents do it? he asked. The man from the First Main Directorate looked at him as if he were nuts.

"You can't trust agents with something like that," he said curtly. "Only your own men. Communists. With experience. The Party Committee of the Residency approved the candidates. Crystal-pure comrades."

The spy hesitated, as if he had gabbed too much. He puffed himself up, straightened, adjusted the lapel of his jacket with its anniversary badge, radiating confidence that only the purest Communist, tested and retested by the Party, could paint a swastika on a wall with black oil paint and not get splattered.

An awkward silence fell on the conference room; Lenin and Dzerzhinsky peered down from the walls, and Lenin seemed to be squinting nastily.

"Let's move on to the next question, comrades," said the deputy chairman.

Later, at the drinking session, which had moved smoothly from the restaurant to the house of one of the locals—the party was for colonels and below, the generals had eaten elsewhere—he went out on the balcony for a smoke and saw a previously opened can of paint with a tattered brush on the lid. The comrade had recently gotten the apartment and was remodeling. Korol barely restrained himself from lifting the dried-on lid with a penknife, dipping the brush into the paint, and decorating the brick wall with just six strokes— the swastika—just to see what it was like, what happened to you if you did it.

Other smokers burst in, chasing away the moment. The next day he came back here, to this office. And he imagined swastikas; they appeared in the wallpaper patterns, in the ceiling cracks, in the toilet tilework, in the window frames, in the ventilation grids beneath the ceiling.

The general looked around. The lines of objects shuddered, and in the unevenness of the plaster beneath the wallpaper and in the squares of the dropped ceiling it appeared, angular, four-armed, capturing your eye with the stark power of the evil symbol.

He remembered a black-and-white photograph: the building of the district center, two-storied, brick, recognizable, surrounded by poplars, flying a flag with a swastika. It hung freely, somehow naturally, as if it had always been there. The flag was flying and the guard stood in front: a small figure in field gray. Major Anikin, the mentor, liked to show the photo to young officers, newbies. As if it were a historical document, evidence of our glorious history: they had captured it, but we threw them out and raised our red flag once again. In fact, Anikin was bitterly mocking: he was taking his revenge for his stagnation, for the fact that no one wanted to replace him in this posting, the operational supervision of the mines and most importantly of Shaft 3/4.

Seeing the photo Anikin was holding then, Korol noted the window of his office on the second floor: he wondered what kind of German had been using it.

There was no closed file on the building itself—what for? But going through the archives that dealt with events during the occupation, he gradually assembled the building's history; he solved it like a puzzle.

It was built as a workers' school before the revolution, then it was taken by the VChK secret police. Korol's office, second floor, left wing, third door on the right, facing the street, room No. 23, was always for the officer in charge of the mine. VChK, OGPU, NKVD—it was here, within these walls, that they invented charges of sabotage, Trotskyite nests, conspiracies spreading through all the levels of the mines. Below, in the cellar, in the interrogation cells, these conspiracies took on flesh on paper, in confessions. When the Soviet troops were retreating, the remaining prisoners were shot there, in the cellar. The cells remained, by the way: under Andropov they were cleaned and painted, new cots were installed, peepholes in each door.

The Germans naturally took over this building. In the right wing, the Gestapo; in the left, the field gendarmerie and a division of the Einsatzkommando. His office was used by Walter Brush, head of the command—that information was known from underground reports. Later, when the Jews were slaughtered and the Einsatzkommando left, an officer moved in who was to guarantee the safety of the mine: the Germans were trying to get the coal operations going and to force the miners to work.

His name apparently was Koenig. King. Like Korol. Also King.

Ha-ha.

They didn't have time to destroy their agent records when they retreated, and Koenig used them. The remaining agents who used to report on anti-Soviet activities now worked for him and reported on anti-German ones. In the cellar, in the interrogation cells, Koenig tortured miners to learn who had sabotaged equipment, the way the Soviets had been torturing people a few years before him.

Part of Koenig's operational materials survived. He kept them, without any shame, in files labeled "NKVD Case No. . . . " A lot of file folders had been delivered in 1941. The general read German; it was his second language at the upper school. He could study and evaluate them. There were no serious underground organizations at the mines. Almost all the underground members still left in 1941 were named by the agents; they didn't have to look for them. But Koenig, no fool, invented an underground and fought it for two years.

He invented it so well, so convincingly, that after the war our people had to immortalize his version, erect a monument to them and open a museum.

The Germans had been here for two years. Those two years didn't seem like much, they came and went.

But it was enough for the building to acquire a ghostly shadow hinting at the resemblance between the siblings in profession. Koenig, incidentally, fleeing hastily in September 1943, also did not have time to destroy his agent cards. The Chekists took them, shuffled them, arresting some and leaving others to keep working. And this was the case, by the way, in hundreds of other places where the Germans had occupied buildings, offices, and cellars of the NKVD, and then returned them to the previous owners, as if it had been a loan.

Koenig—Korol, Korol—Koenig.

This building had waited for him, a hospitable house, its doors open to all, Nazis and Communists. It didn't care which flag, which service. As long as blood flowed. Senior Lieutenant Zadovsky, who in 1937 sat in office No. 23 and compiled execution lists for the mines, was himself arrested and executed in 1937, in December. His successor, Lieutenant Mikulchenko, was shot in April 1938. Prosecutor Rudenko, who as part of the troika approved the lists, later in Nuremberg blamed the Nazis—what a joke; even Goebbels couldn't have come up with that.

The general looked around again. The lines of objects shuddered once again, more persistently this time. Silhouettes of swastikas floated up from the depths of the walls, appearing in the shadows.

Have to get out of here, he thought. Others can clean the field. You can't get rid of all the witnesses, and the military won't give up their own, anyway. The SAM team was already home in the barracks. But the ones who received the Omela and showed them the target, the "militiamen," had to be taken out. With that thought, the sense of power returned to him; but the sense of evil swirling around him did not disappear.

Enough for today, time to clear his head.

. . . They got to the Paradise by nine. The general liked the joint. It used to be a canteen in Soviet times: they had put away a lot of macaroni and chopped meat cutlets there. Rather, what he liked was the swindling owner's business sense; he was first to realize that the new regime was going to last, even though most of the locals treated it like a bandit raid, not expecting it to still be in place by summer. But this cunning guy, the first swallow, figured out what was happening and quickly refurnished his already vulgar tavern, brought in mirrored glass, fake granite, drooping chandeliers, stuffed leather furniture, palm trees, in just two weeks, and changed the sign. It used to be Pasha's and now it was the Paradise, shiny and fancy; he even brought in a chef from Europe, Neapolitan cuisine or some such. The so-called militiamen were averse to it but eventually ate it up, you can't fight glamor.

Only three or four people knew the general at the Paradise, Monk and the other chieftains. The rest, hustlers and brainless baboons, sensed his importance and avoided him. He had his own table, in an alcove: it was more comfortable for him and more convenient for his guards. They came in the back way, through the kitchen. The general recalled how the canteen reeked of boiled vegetables since for some reason they often served stuffed cabbage to the miners, and now it was shrimp and steak.

Something was going on in the restaurant; the baboons were tense, eyeing one another. They were at odds about something. A white dress flashed by. *Cherchez la femme*, they were divvying up a woman, then. What kind of fool would bring a beauty here if he didn't know how to stand up for himself?

There he was, by the window, sulking, the face slightly familiar. *Click, click* in his memory Rolodex. He looked like the neighbor of Marianna, aka Snow White; that tall explosives miner, they had a two-family house, so the neighbors got into the surveillance photos sometimes. A young "militiaman." Judging by his uniform, in Monk's unit. They all had similar camo outfits from the same warehouse.

He didn't need to order; the fawning waiters knew his taste. He was finally feeling good, in the midst of the Pithecanthropus, scum who would never understand the wines on the menu.

Suddenly the light show and music came on, the mirrored ball began turning, scattering silver specks, with Modern Talking singing, "*La-la-la*, you're my heart, you're my soul."

The general was stunned. The damned owner knew, and all the baboon leaders knew, that there was no music while he was there. No Soviet gangster chanson, no disco crap. The bedlam began only after he left, and not before. Semyon, his loyal dog, sensed his chief's unhappiness and rose to shut them up.

But the men were swept off the dance floor, and the woman in the white dress stepped into the circle.

At first, the general saw only her smile: a scarlet flower, a specter of color that could not exist here, in the gray-black town covered with coal dust from the slag heap.

He imagined that there was other music playing through Modern Talking, through the caramel voices. Violins? What instruments were they? Maybe not even instruments?

The thin metal of the fuselage groaned and tore. The turbines squealed, grated, choked. Air roared into the cabin. People screamed in hundreds of voices. The plane screamed as it was ripped apart. It all turned into not-music.

Vertigo.

Falling.

Breaking clouds.

A smile. A red slash. Behind it a figure in white, dancing but not quite a dance, not following the song's rhythm, not repeating movements, pushing away from the walls of the men's circle, as narrow as a well, as a mine shaft, splashing herself around the room with the predeath foam of a captured mermaid. Oh, now he recognized that troubling, inexpressible whiteness.

The whitest white.

White. He came one evening to the surveillance point across from Marianna's house. They had a telescope, a ridiculous piece of equipment on a tripod. In the lens aimed at the window, Snow White was dancing. Dancing with herself. The dance was like a performance, a pantomime, because in it Snow White was water, foam, working hands, and the resulting cleanliness.

He felt shame and lust. He wanted to take her by force so that the whiteness, loving and alien, with a secret power, would dim, turn pale, dead, docile. That night he ordered the surveillance shut down. He could not allow those stupid ensigns to see her day after day.

And there she was dancing, the young Snow White. Her daughter, definitely her daughter, who had not been born when he left for Moscow. The kid by the window had brought her. The general felt powerful jealousy, as he had for the ensigns, for the unsuccessful lover.

Scarlet lips. Snow White had never used lipstick, the general remembered. She had no makeup at all, he had discovered during an illegal search of the house.

Scarlet lips. A chance to replay those days, that impossibility, that impotence.

The girl was dancing. The general imagined how the baboons would grumble and bare their teeth when he took her away. She was teasing them with her purity, and every man was anticipating what he would do to her. Why had she ever come here, the brat must not have understood where he had taken her, she would be found later in the woods, or never found again.

The general beckoned Monk with a finger. He came over,

still squinting at the dancer over his shoulder. The general asked who the youngster was by the window. When Monk told him that he was a former policeman from the Moscow special regiment, a local who had guided the Omela, the general was astounded by how well the cards had fallen. Monk, no fool, understood everything, noting how the general had shaken his head at the word *Omela*.

Hesitating, he still said cautiously, "His uncle is the deputy commander of the special regiment."

The general merely spread his hands, showing that he understood and sympathized, but there was nothing he could do: orders. He watched Monk send two of his men to take the boy away. He imagined they told him, We have to hurry, meet a truck, this is important, and the boy went with them, the boy had no idea that these two men were Monk's specialists for such situations. They would make it look like a death in a shoot-out, and no uncle, even if he was a cop five times over, would prove otherwise. Most importantly, it was all within the bounds of his authority and assignment. Nothing personal.

The mirrored doors of the Paradise shut behind the boy and his companions.

"Bring her," the general told Semyon. He was certain that the "militiamen" would not dare argue. But he allowed a ten percent chance that someone would object. Someone low in the pecking order, a novice, a punk.

But even they said nothing when Semyon led her away. They went back to the tables, swearing, and some went outside with their bottles.

She sat before him, and he could see nothing besides her scarlet smile, besides her lips. He wanted to suck the red mouth.

"What's your name?" he asked.

"Zhanna."

Marianna, Zhanna... The ladies who visited Snow White also had unusual names, Teresia, Isabella, Violetta, like a club with foreign members.

She radiated the heat of the dance. Thin, she seemed to have lost a kilogram dancing.

Marianna's eyes.

Marianna's hands.

Scarlet lips. As if from a stranger's face.

"Let's go," he said, and he took her hand.

She rose obediently and followed.

Semyon started the car and drove away—and then, just fifty meters or so later, braked.

The street was blocked by the young men from the militia who had left the bar. They amused themselves this way, setting up roadblocks at night, stopping cars and demanding money.

The girl sat next to him on the backseat, silent, breathing deeply, and her breathing and docility, as if she were stoned, aroused the general.

Semyon blasted the horn and pushed with the bumper.

The militiamen, belonging to Boba, would not disperse. They were drunk, mean drunk. Pretended not to know whose car it was.

It was Zhanna who had intoxicated them. But they would be left there on the road, and he would make love to her. That thought aroused the general even more. He opened the door and got out to curse them out properly, to make their ears rattle.

A fool started to raise his automatic to shoot into the air; they enjoyed that, there were fireworks every night. But another one drunkenly bumped into his hand, and the barrel made a crooked arc, spurting bullets.

The general was hit in the chest.

He was falling, falling, falling into a black shaft that had no bottom, and somewhere in the distance a black dog barked and barked, both of its heads barked.

THE ENGINEER

The missile.

Its instantaneous flight, its crushing impact.

The multiplicity of deaths inherent in its very idea.

The missile looked so modernist, so eerily elegant: a militaristic fetish of purpose and expediency.

It looked abstract and, I would even say, sterile, conceptual: the barefaced idea of a targeted attack embodied in sheer metal form. A child of science, a product of the technological chain.

But I see the connections.

I know the hidden genealogies of things.

All the rockets of the world share a common link in their family tree.

. . . The Nazis could have come here, to the East, by land. In cars and trains and horse-drawn carriages. They could reach it on foot in marching columns. Defeat Soviet troops. Starve the prisoners of war. Exterminate the Jews.

But the Wehrmacht could not land in England, which had won the battle for the English Channel. They could not send in the Einsatzgruppen. Or terrify the English into giving up their intended victims for slaughter.

And then a new weapon was born: the long arm of death, capable of reaching across the channel. A perfect form, a shark of the air, an apparatus without a man inside. The fruit of vain anger and desire for revenge. An expression of hatred of life, of murderous power over space.

It was the V-2, the *Vergeltungswaffe*, the weapon of vengeance, the child of the failed Blitzkrieg, the scourge of nations—the womb from which all the missiles in the world originated. Concentrated violence like an injection that could be administered remotely, without conquering territory, without building concentration camps.

V-2s fell for years: several thousand missiles. Several thousand deaths. Revenge for revenge's sake. For the sake of fear and terror. Expensive, absurd vengeance: I think Speer wrote that because of the priority accorded the V-2, the Nazis did not produce antiaircraft missiles that could have defended Germany.

When we were being killed in the spring of 1942, it was being manufactured, tested, prepared. It was built by forced laborers: the living dead. So that it could make other people dead.

Like the ancient monsters of myths, who came into the world from the caves, from the deep shelters of the earth, it was born in the darkness, in the long and deep tunnels of the subterranean forced labor camp Mittelbau-Dora in the foothills of the Harz. Thirty kilometers south of Brocken, the mountain of witches' sabbaths, which people for centuries considered to be the seat of the forces of pagan evil, dwelling in dark cellars and ravines, in the subconscious of Christian Europe.

Yes, the V-2 was literally created in underground forges as a weapon of the underworld, a weapon of the Titans or Jötunns of the chthonic earth threatening the heavens.

Both the Soviets and the Allies brought out the documentation for the V-2, brought out the scientists. Therefore, they also brought out the doom, the sin of its creation, now sleeping in each of the new missiles.

The downed passenger plane could have served as a warning. A wake-up call. But it would only bolster the zombies in their sense of impunity. Their thirst for revenge against a world that had dared to sideline them.

And the day was not far off when more missiles would fly.

After all, they, the zombies, had deep arsenals, once filled for the doomsday of World War III.

And missiles lived a long time and aged very slowly.

Like sharks.

Alas, that day was not far off, and the young White Lady had to face it. If she could defeat the temptation sent to her. Recognize the devil's trick. A mocking gift to a pure creature unaware of its purity.

Lipstick. Oh, there was a lot of room for interpretation. In the Middle Ages, it was the sign of a prostitute. During the Renaissance, it was a symbol of revived corporeality—one might say, rehabilitated, no longer taboo.

But here, now, it was the kiss of war and the communion of lies.

The girl still hated her mother for the way she died. Still felt betrayed. And wanted the other, the old pure mother back. She thought that that one, mired in dirt and worthlessness, was no longer Marianna.

This was the main lie that kept the daughter from accepting the horror and suffering of her mother's disgusting death, which had stolen her dignity but still belonged to her and had been experienced by her, her own personal death, inseparable from her to the very end.

We are happy to subconsciously shift the blame to the dead person, to the victim, because it was she who made a mistake somewhere, who angered fate, who allowed her death to be long, unkempt, staining everything around her, who became a capricious monster tormenting her relatives.

But in reality, of course, we commit the betrayal. Because we don't realize what we've been sent. What we are meant to see.

In the hopelessness of the agony and the gruesome details of dying, in becoming a blackening mummy that was draining the internal hemorrhage, death comes to our cozy, lovely home that is no match for it.

It was the death of the age of mass murder. The death of concentration camps. The death of war, famine, epidemics. It's the death of the starving prisoners dumped under the lower bunks. Or those who fell into a mine shaft unscathed, alive. When it was not far to fall, because the mine was almost full.

This was the death of all those who were rejected, tossed out of memory, squeezed into unmarked graves. So it appeared to people of other generations.

The war, before it had even begun, had already crushed the White Lady. And she only had time to speak to her daughter in the language of her own death, the language of her own decay, to offer herself as the only possible testimony explaining what the White Ladies did. What they scrubbed away in this world.

But war, the font of all loot and trophies, had thrown the girl a lipstick: redraw, rewrite yourself, and a miracle would happen. You would be free in your destiny. But to be free, you needed this insignificant, even apologetic measure of complicity: to use a dead person's object that had fallen into your hands as if by chance.

I don't know everything. But I remember the temptation of her grandmother: silk lingerie and the dress of a dead German woman, an aristocrat. The lieutenant who raped and murdered her took the things from her closet—in case he wanted to bed a self-respecting lady.

I feel she has a future, but I can't see into it.

And I can't help her. I am not a guide, a secret mentor, or hidden spirit counselor. None of the imaginary creatures who support and direct the hero. These creatures abound in fairy tales where the other side appears as a second, separate reality where the magic originates.

I am limited to the role of witness turned into testimony. The role of a black box that signals the location of a catastrophe and records its blow.

But my testimony is rejected.

When that big mine collapse happened, a whole shift

died, talk spread through the town: they shouldn't have opened up the works leading in the direction of Shaft 3/4. The KGB had closed them just in case, forbade working them, even though the coal there was first-class and the seams barely touched. But there was no one to tell the new owners they couldn't open them up.

Yes, there were signs there: the cage jammed during the descent, the lanterns in the lantern room were not filled. But they checked the methane level: it was as low as could be, no danger. It wasn't the methane that was the danger. The mine cut into a zone with depressurized rock. The coal looked strong, but in fact it was rotten, grated by pressure. It sagged when they started to pick out the seam; it fell like sunflower seeds from a burst bag.

Yes, there were signs. But we didn't send them. They were sent to the miners by their own intuition, their experience of mining, which warned them of the impending danger and shed the infrared light of their sixth sense onto ordinary events that were perfectly capable of serving as an alarm. Our alleged ability to "answer," to defend ourselves, to prevent our afterlife from being disturbed is only a reflection of an underlying, innate willingness to reject us, to prevent us from coming to your world.

We did not respond. We cannot respond in any way, in any way at all. We have no power over the earth strata, over the forces of tectonics.

Power is exactly what has been taken away from us absolutely.

When people speak of the supernatural, the first thing they think about is power. One that violates the physical laws. That comes from itself. The supernatural as super knowledge, the ability to see future and past, pass through walls, change images, control elements, move mountains, kill and revive with a look—that's what you like. You like wizards, magi, dark tyrants enslaving nations to do evil and light warriors who break their spells. An imaginary parallel world in which the supernatural acts, fights, transforms, and creates.

But our authentic supernaturalism lies, so to speak, on the minus side of the scale. Yes, it can be felt and experienced. As absolute powerlessness.

As an absence, a withdrawal from life.

In other words, we're more about subtraction than addition.

If anyone who as a child felt a deep horror when solving arithmetic problems, a horror at their disciplined, unreasoning brutality, if he asked himself why exactly eight minus three, why exactly these three and where were they, what was wrong with them, if he heard the secret cry of the subtracted apples, carrots, dolls, books, watermelons going nowhere, into the abyss, he has the ability to hear us, the absent ones.

Our supernaturalism is the inability to ethically explain what has happened to us.

Our supernaturalism is that there are too many of us, and we are here with you, petrified, fused into a single thing that has no name.

There is no language to describe us. Language will say that we have become stone, but it cannot convey the extent of our detachment, our effacement, our oblivion.

The Nazis killed us.

They killed us so that we would disappear, so that the memory of us would never revive, so that our existence would be erased, so that not a sound or a letter of us would remain.

The Soviets, who defeated the Nazis, have carried out their will. Deprived us of the last grace of sacrifice—not vengeance, but testimony—killed us after death.

You have dozens of ways to imagine the presence of the dead. Sometimes you think you see your deceased grandparents at the end of the dacha path, like when you were a child and they went to the village to get groceries. Looking at the things of the departed, you feel close to them. Clearing the cemetery plot in spring of the branches that fell during the winter, painting the fence and the bench, you think that they, dwelling invisibly here, are watching you, and you try to paint evenly and in two layers, otherwise your late grandfather, a very precise man, will be dissatisfied.

True, as a rule, it's your own dead.

But we, a fragment of the destroyed tribe, left without relatives, without leaders and intercessors, who were also destroyed—we belong to you, too. We have no possibility of arising in the minds of our descendants, for we have no descendants. We, as complete orphans, can only appeal to *urbi et orbi*, and—if you don't find it too presumptuous—everyone is responsible for us.

One day, when the zombies are defeated, when it is time to rebuild what has been destroyed, then, as you sort through the ruins of war, you will one day find us.

A deposit of humans.

DAY FIVE

ZHANNA

She awoke feeling a fly had crawled over her lip.

She ran her finger over it—no, nothing, her imagination.

But there was something wrong with her lips.

Some kind of plaque? An inflammation? And there was a strange smell. As if she had been teasing a wild animal, a predator, through the bars of the cage, and it had blown the rank odor of its breath on her.

But where, who, what?

She remembered nothing.

She got in the shower—hurry, the closer to noon, the more likely the water would be turned off. She soaped up with a sponge. She suddenly sensed that she was washing with strange, unfamiliar movements: starting in the wrong place, continuing in the wrong direction, touching herself the wrong way. Reflexively, she tried to wash away the strangeness, rinsed, but it did not leave. On the contrary, it clung to her more tightly.

Her body hurt.

Muscles, cartilage, joints, vertebrae ached as if she had been tortured on the rack yesterday.

Yesterday...

The bright dance floor.

She seemed to be defending it, claiming it.

A multieyed, multiarmed monster lurked, waiting for the protective shield of the dance to fall so it could reach out with its paw to grab her and take her away.

As if dancing, she took a few steps back in memory. She saw herself and Valet at the table at the Paradise. But she couldn't remember wanting to dance. She remembered getting up, knowing that the dangerous and lusting men had to be mesmerized, sedated, distracted. Her body started dancing on its own. The dance appeared like a djinn, elementally. It danced her, a dance with no name. It continued in her when she got into the car. Tore her out of the bullet-riddled jeep. Gave incredible lightness to her feet: run, run! Deftly threw her into alleyways, moved branches from her face, silenced the barking dogs, showed her the shortest way as she ran through the coal-black night.

Dance, dance . . . But what had happened before that?

Zhanna got out of the shower.

Her naked skin was burned by odors, as if her entire body had the sense of smell.

The house reeked of disease and filth. The water in the neighbor's well stank of slime. From all four sides came the stench of death in the forests and fields, valleys and gardens, the ruins of mine buildings, diggings, mine dumps, vegetable gardens; the still unlocated bodies were rotting in the heat, faces as yellow as the bellies of watermelons.

The stench of decay enveloped her in a sticky shroud,

settling on her skin, making it itch. She rushed back to the bathroom, turned the shower on full, but the metal sunflower showerhead merely belched and released a thin yellow dribble, sour and warm, like baby piss.

With it, all the filth of the last months poured onto Zhanna. Everything that could not be washed away, yellow brown. Bitter saliva filled her mouth.

Where to get clean water to rinse her mouth? She glanced at the mirror.

On her pale face—pink, bitten lips. The lipstick had worn off, its red color gone, but the smile seemed glued on. Unnatural. Not living. Like that of a corpse.

Where was the lipstick?

She had to color her lips.

Return the bright red.

Return the smile to life.

Go off to dance again.

The stench of decay grew stronger.

As if her mother were still there, decomposing in the bed where she had died. She lay in the bushes. In the plants. In the groves of gnarled oaks. In the beds of dried-up streams. In dumps, barns, garages. They were searching for her, but they couldn't gather up all of her, in the multitude of all her bodies, and the scorching sun burned down, and the mine crows also searched.

The lipstick.

She had to put it on. Return to the Paradise. Dance again, enchant again.

Her bag was empty. Zhanna remembered that it got caught on a shrub yesterday. Not far at all. The lipstick was in the grass there. Just playing games with her.

Zhanna touched the doorknob. But her feet would not move. The smile she had seen in the mirror was looming before her inner gaze and she could not tell who was smiling: she, reflected in the mirror, or some other woman on the other side of the mirror.

"When you don't know what choice to make, clean house," her mother had taught her. "While you're cleaning, the decision will come to you. Just don't be lazy!"

Zhanna, angrily parodying her mother's advice, grabbed a mop and swept it dry across the floor, chasing the dust from corner to corner. Strangely, the mop in her hands calmed her down.

No longer sarcastic, but still smiling at her silly idea, she brought the dusty floor mats outside. She got her mother's big trough from the storeroom. She brought up the linens from her mother's bed that she had thrown in the cellar. They were dried out and stuck together into a smelly clump. In the daylight, it looked as if the fabric could never be clean: the filth had been absorbed so deeply that it had become part of the textile.

Zhanna threw it into the trough. She smiled at her forgetfulness: there wasn't any water. The water pump would probably not work until evening. She picked up the crumpled hose, turned the clamped valve. The hose filled, snorted, spat out black scraps, and then spurted the cleanest icy water.

No longer surprised, Zhanna soaked the sheets and then brought out all the fabrics that had borne witness to the disease: tablecloths, curtains, towels, rags, nightgowns. Soiled and wrinkled, they lay in a mound under the blazing sun, a slag heap of suffering, imprinted with scars and stains: yellow, brown, red. They had the same vile, wretched smell as the space around her, the fields, ravines, and groves. Zhanna stood in front of the mound, not believing that it could all be washed. Feeling a mounting stubbornness, the desire to resist, as she had at the dance, to clean at least a scrap. Feeling that if she cleaned even a bit, she would do something for the greater good. For all the dead in the area, past and new, some of whom could still not be found.

Zhanna took her mother's washboard. Ran her fingers along the wavy ribs. The board, dried and cracked with disuse—her mother always used a wooden board; she said wood was gentler on the fabric—responded, trembled under her fingers.

She did not notice time vanish. How she became water and foam, the splash and slap of the roller. Iridescent, sparkling, glowing foam that rose in the trough like bread dough and never ran out. How the stench and decay disappeared. And how the long-forgotten, sharp, fine smell of cleanliness appeared.

When she came to, the foam was still bubbling, gurgling in the trough. The drained water had flowed down the ditch. And all around, on the line and on bushes, sheets and duvet covers were drying under the scorching sun, blinding with Marianna's cleanliness that was deeper and brighter than whiteness.

She gathered them, feeling the primordiality of the fabrics with her weary, painfully sensitive fingertips. On the stove, she heated up her mother's favorite iron, made of heavy cast-iron, its nose like a battleship from an old movie. And began ironing, filling the house with the smell of red-hot iron, heated fibers, hissing steam. Ironing, imprinting the fabric with purity. Smoothing out the wrinkles and creases. Aligning corners and seams. Creating that geometric, calibrated precision that completed the transformation under her mother's hands, the rebirth of washed things.

Things took their places in the closets. Zhanna felt that something she had no name for had been restored. Something more than just order or just cleanliness. Compounded of the two, but not equal to them.

She scraped the floors. Washed and wiped dishes and cutlery, remembering what and how her mother had served in those plates, bowls. Wiped down shelves and cabinets.

Stopping at last, feeling the renewal of her home, she was suddenly frightened. It seemed to her that by restoring cleanliness she had unwittingly destroyed a memory, erased the last traces of her mother's sorrowful presence.

But she saw that in fact it was her mother's presence that was restored. And dying, in all its nauseating details, was no longer frightening, the way a festering wound does not repel a nurse.

Just recently, Zhanna had been tormented by the fact that her mother had done everything right in her life, and that correctness had not saved her. But now she saw her mother not as an accidental victim, thrown into torment. But as a soldier, a guardian, fallen at her post.

This thought—that her mother had been killed, died in battle—made Zhanna realize what awareness she had been forced to push away from herself when her mother's torment, the daily, minute-by-minute, exhausting necessity of caring for a patient who was losing her mind, had cut her off from the world; when it had imprisoned her in the house, in the corridors of a particular routine that involuntary caregivers walk, corridors of unhappiness, separating her from other people, generating an underlying shame that this happened to her. She had not realized that war had come.

In the duration of her mother's agony, in the depth of her suffering, Zhanna, who knew about war only from history class at school, could only guess the scale of the war, its power over the future.

War.

She said the word aloud.

The war had a face: yesterday's crowd in the restaurant, a multiarmed and multieyed monster.

Zhanna saw it now as if in slow motion. She heard what its mouths were saying to each other, but she didn't understand.

In their house they spoke Russian, laced with words from the borderlands and local miners' jargon. The military spoke Russian, too. But this Russian was like the language of a man possessed. As if all the meanings of words were mixed up, and good in this language meant evil, peace meant war, justice meant crime, truth meant lies, black meant white, freedom meant slavery. Her mother, when the disease dug its claws into her, spoke in this language: Fascist . . . Zhanna felt an unclean spirit, as if she had approached a cage with a man-eating bear, its matted fur covered in blood.

She recoiled.

She heard the ticking of the clock. It seemed to intensify. *Tick-tock.*

They're looking for you.

Time snapped, raced on.

The many-headed beast must be looking for her. The cause of last night's shooting. Valet could tell them, but he must have been silent since they had not come for her yet. They've been going door-to-door, asking around. But so far, no luck. No one wanted to help them. Her mother's work had not been in vain. Evil succeeded in far from everything here; it fumbled blindly, and Zhanna was protected by a thin shield of noncompliance: no, haven't seen her, she didn't run past, we go to bed early, didn't hear anything yesterday.

But the protection couldn't last forever.

Soon time would run out.

She didn't know anyone outside the settlement who could help. Where she could hide. She couldn't even just pick a target.

Kharkiv? Kyiv?

Anywhere.

She suddenly felt the strange freedom of this state. She realized she had been wrong thinking that her mother was bound to the mine by the very essence of her service.

It was her own choice, not shackles, not chains.

Surrendering to ignorance, to aimlessness, she walked around the house, memorizing its cleanliness. That was what they would find—the shiny floors and the ironed, terrifying whiteness of the linens: like a message they would never be able to decipher.

She found her father's old miner's headlamp in the closet, the one they'd taken off the body when they went through the rubble. The flashlight, designed to withstand the impact, hadn't broken, and the mine rescuers had seen that ray of light coming from under the debris.

Her mother had used it when the power went out. An electrician in the mine shops gutted the battery box and inserted terminals for batteries.

Zhanna flicked a switch and the flashlight lit up welcomingly, as if glad to be remembered. She packed her father's backpack he used when he went fishing. She put in money, passport, a change of underwear and clothes, medicines, phone, power bank, synthetic flabby sleeping bag, also from her father's fishing equipment, his homemade knife, his flask.

She couldn't remember him. She was in the womb when he died. Didn't feel connected to him. In the mining town, death in the mine was not considered something special: there were cave-ins, accidents, methane emissions. Here, everyone knew that one day a miner might not return from a shift.

But now touching his things, she felt that this calmness that surprised her, this scrupulous and precise choice of things for escape, this readiness to do with very little, was not from Marianna; it came from him, unknown, chosen by her mother, protecting his child, leaving her an inheritance she only now understood.

As she left, she covered the mirror, leaving in it the reflection of her face, her lips without a single scarlet spot. She strode down the path to the wicket gate, feeling that everything here was done. She might never see home again. Or she would, but in another life.

Night found her behind the ruins of the mine, behind the slag heap. She was afraid to light a lantern: something was rustling in the darkness, either people or animals. She looked for a place to lay her sleeping bag, and suddenly she felt a draft of underground cold in the warmth of the night.

It was the abandoned diggings breathing. Zhanna went down the steep slope inside and lit the light. The passage was narrow, almost her height, the old bracing made of unsheathed logs sawn in these woods was rotten and sagging, and under her feet, pieces of wretched earthy coal from the ceiling. But Zhanna felt that today the dig would not give out, would protect her, would shelter her for the night.

As she fell asleep, she saw Graz, the town-by-the-hill as it had appeared to her one day after Christmas.

Oh, the town was empty, as empty as could be, as if all the inhabitants were gone. Hidden in the hill. And the hill, though stone, faintly rose and fell, giving away their suppressed breaths. But why were they hiding?

On the streets, only the occasional tourist, as if the town had forgotten to warn them of danger. They seemed to be lured by the military museum in the town hall.

Zhanna slipped through, joining someone else's tour. She was lost among a thousand spades, swords, halberds, gisarmes, outlandish weapons that looked like ghastly metal flowers whose petal shape was determined by the method of killing. There were mannequins wearing armor, creating iron men, and even an iron horse carrying a warrior in tournament armor.

The metal men seemed capable of coming to life. Especially with the stomp of an excursion on the wooden floors above: as if in a siege with reinforcements rushing to the battle, running over the decks of the fortress wall. Were the inhabitants hiding from them, the iron-armed ones, knowing that one day a year they wake up?

Zhanna hurried there, to the protection of the hill. On the way she passed the crystal palace of the department store. They were dismantling the window displays. Sleek, submissive mannequins, yesterday's perfect people in luxurious outfits, lay naked in the strange, accidental, and yet not accidental poses they were left in by workers who had stripped them of their clothes.

Zhanna had almost run into the tunnel leading to the

elevator, to the underground railroad for tourists, to the concert hall in the mountain . . .

When the lights went out.

And inside the mountain, as on a black screen, she began to make out another huge underground, illuminated by the ghostly rays of headlamps, candles, kerosene lamps, similar to the first firelight in the first caves of mankind, where the first people took refuge from the evil of the night.

A vast underground into which a whole country had descended. Tunnels and basements, mines, subway lines full of people. Where orchestras played and babies were born, where surgeons operated and teachers taught. Where flickered that strange illumination, the light of vigils, the light of prayers: lanterns, flashlights, candles.

And in the sky above them, as dark as anthracite, rockets flew, setting off the air-raid sirens.

Zhanna couldn't see them all, but she knew there were dozens. Embedded in their inanimate electronic brains were targets that the living mind refused to accept: apartment buildings, power plants, shopping centers, city squares.

Zhanna knew her exact place in the future.

There, in the subterranean land where the bandages of the wounded and the diapers of newborns must be washed.

Potsdam, 2023

SERGEI LEBEDEV was born in Moscow in 1981 and worked for seven years on geological expeditions in northern Russia and Central Asia. Lebedev is a poet, essayist, and journalist. His novels have been translated into twenty languages and have received great acclaim in the English-speaking world. *The New York Review of Books* has hailed Lebedev as "the best of Russia's younger generation of writers."

ANTONINA W. BOUIS is one of the leading translators of Russian literature working today. She has translated over eighty works from authors such as Evgeny Yevtushenko, Mikhail Bulgakov, Andrei Sakharov, Sergei Dovlatov, and Arkady and Boris Strugatsky.

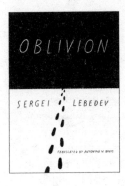

OBLIVION
BY SERGEI LEBEDEV

In one of the first 21st century Russian novels to probe the legacy of the Soviet prison camp system, a young man travels to the vast wastelands of the Far North to uncover the truth about a shadowy neighbor who saved his life, and whom he knows only as Grandfather II. Emerging from today's Russia, where the ills of the past are being forcefully erased from public memory, this masterful novel represents an epic literary attempt to rescue history from the brink of oblivion.

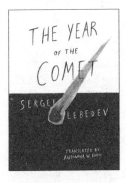

THE YEAR OF THE COMET
BY SERGEI LEBEDEV

A story of a Russian boyhood and coming of age as the Soviet Union is on the brink of collapse. Lebedev depicts a vast empire coming apart at the seams, transforming a very public moment into something tender and personal, and writes with stunning beauty and shattering insight about childhood and the growing consciousness of a boy in the world.

UNTRACEABLE
BY SERGEI LEBEDEV

An extraordinary Russian novel about poisons of all kinds: physical, moral and political. Professor Kalitin is a ruthless, narcissistic chemist who has developed an untraceable lethal poison called Neophyte while working in a secret city on an island in the Russian far east. When the Soviet Union collapses, he defects to the West in a riveting tale through which Lebedev probes the ethical responsibilities of scientists providing modern tyrants with ever newer instruments of retribution and control.

THE GOOSE FRITZ
BY SERGEI LEBEDEV

This revelatory novel shows why Karl Ove
Knausgaard has likened its celebrated Russian
author to an "indomitable . . . animal that won't
let go of something when it gets its teeth into it."
The book tells the story of a young Russian named
Kirill, the sole survivor of a once numerous clan
of German origin, who delves relentlessly into the
unresolved past. *The Goose Fritz* illuminates both
personal and political history in a passion-filled
family saga about an often confounding country that has long fascinated
the world.

A PRESENT PAST
BY SERGEI LEBEDEV

The Soviet and post-Soviet world, with its untold
multitude of crimes, is a natural breeding ground
for ghost stories. No one writes them more
movingly than Russian author Sergei Lebedev,
who in this stunning volume probes a collective
guilty conscience marked by otherworldliness and
the denial of misdeeds. These eleven tales share
a mystical topography in which the legacy of
totalitarian regimes is ever-present.

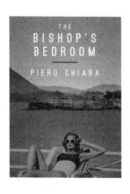

THE BISHOP'S BEDROOM
BY PIERO CHIARA

World War Two has just come to an end and there's
a yearning for renewal. A man in his thirties is
sailing on Lake Maggiore in northern Italy, hoping
to put off the inevitable return to work. Dropping
anchor in a small, fashionable port, he meets the
enigmatic owner of a nearby villa. The two form
an uneasy bond, recognizing in each other a shared
taste for idling and erotic adventure. A sultry,
stylish psychological thriller executed with supreme
literary finesse.

THE EYE
BY PHILIPPE COSTAMAGNA

It's a rare and secret profession, comprising a few dozen people around the world equipped with a mysterious mixture of knowledge and innate sensibility. Summoned to Swiss bank vaults, Fifth Avenue apartments, and Tokyo storerooms, they are entrusted by collectors, dealers, and museums to decide if a coveted picture is real or fake and to determine if it was painted by Leonardo da Vinci or Raphael. *The Eye* lifts the veil on the rarified world of connoisseurs devoted to the authentication and discovery of Old Master artworks.

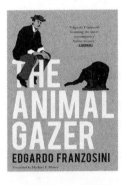

THE ANIMAL GAZER
BY EDGARDO FRANZOSINI

A hypnotic novel inspired by the strange and fascinating life of sculptor Rembrandt Bugatti, brother of the fabled automaker. Bugatti obsessively observes and sculpts the baboons, giraffes, and panthers in European zoos, finding empathy with their plight and identifying with their life in captivity. Rembrandt Bugatti's work, now being rediscovered, is displayed in major art museums around the world and routinely fetches large sums at auction. Edgardo Franzosini recreates the young artist's life with intense lyricism, passion, and sensitivity.

ALLMEN AND THE DRAGONFLIES
BY MARTIN SUTER

Johann Friedrich von Allmen has exhausted his family fortune by living in Old World grandeur despite present-day financial constraints. Forced to downscale, Allmen inhabits the garden house of his former Zurich estate, attended by his Guatemalan butler, Carlos. This is the first of a series of humorous, fast-paced detective novels devoted to a memorable gentleman thief. A thrilling art heist escapade infused with European high culture and luxury that doesn't shy away from the darker side of human nature.

THE MADELEINE PROJECT
BY CLARA BEAUDOUX

A young woman moves into a Paris apartment and discovers a storage room filled with the belongings of the previous owner, a certain Madeleine who died in her late nineties, and whose treasured possessions nobody seems to want. In an audacious act of journalism driven by personal curiosity and humane tenderness, Clara Beaudoux embarks on *The Madeleine Project*, documenting what she finds on Twitter with text and photographs, introducing the world to an unsung 20th century figure.

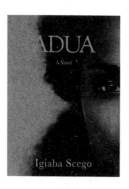

ADUA
BY IGIABA SCEGO

Adua, an immigrant from Somalia to Italy, has lived in Rome for nearly forty years. She came seeking freedom from a strict father and an oppressive regime, but her dreams of film stardom ended in shame. Now that the civil war in Somalia is over, her homeland calls her. She must decide whether to return and reclaim her inheritance, but also how to take charge of her own story and build a future.

THE 6:41 TO PARIS
BY JEAN-PHILIPPE BLONDEL

Cécile, a stylish 47-year-old, has spent the weekend visiting her parents outside Paris. By Monday morning, she's exhausted. These trips back home are stressful and she settles into a train compartment with an empty seat beside her. But it's soon occupied by a man she recognizes as Philippe Leduc, with whom she had a passionate affair that ended in her brutal humiliation 30 years ago. In the fraught hour and a half that ensues, Cécile and Philippe hurtle towards the French capital in a psychological thriller about the pain and promise of past romance.

THE MADONNA OF NOTRE DAME
BY ALEXIS RAGOUGNEAU

Fifty thousand people jam into Notre Dame Cathedral to celebrate the Feast of the Assumption. The next morning, a beautiful young woman clothed in white kneels at prayer in a cathedral side chapel. But when someone accidentally bumps against her, her body collapses. She has been murdered. This thrilling novel illuminates shadowy corners of the world's most famous cathedral, shedding light on good and evil with suspense, compassion and wry humor.

THE LAST WEYNFELDT
BY MARTIN SUTER

Adrian Weynfeldt is an art expert in an international auction house, a bachelor in his mid-fifties living in a grand Zurich apartment filled with costly paintings and antiques. Always correct and well-mannered, he's given up on love until one night—entirely out of character for him—Weynfeldt decides to take home a ravishing but unaccountable young woman and gets embroiled in an art forgery scheme that threatens his buttoned up existence. This refined page-turner moves behind elegant bourgeois facades into darker recesses of the heart.

MOVING THE PALACE
BY CHARIF MAJDALANI

A young Lebanese adventurer explores the wilds of Africa, encountering an eccentric English colonel in Sudan and enlisting in his service. In this lush chronicle of far-flung adventure, the military recruit crosses paths with a compatriot who has dismantled a sumptuous palace and is transporting it across the continent on a camel caravan. This is a captivating modern-day Odyssey in the tradition of Bruce Chatwin and Paul Theroux.

New Vessel Press

To purchase these titles and for more information
please visit newvesselpress.com.